WE RUN

NEW YORK 4

a ghetto game of thrones

written and directed by

Sa'id Salaam

There's only two ways out of the game. Dead or in jail...

Table of Contents

Chapter 1

"Don't worry cuz. I got this down here B," Carlos assured Buddha when he got a chance to speak to him.

"Huh?" Buddha asked and winced since he didn't understand how it pertained to the caskets being lowered into the ground. "What the fuck are you talking about?"

"At a funeral. Your sister's funeral," Tara added since anything that irritated her husband irritated her as well.

"Nah, I'm just saying. We can, yeah..." he stammered and slinked away. He saw one of his sister's friends and slid over to her. "Hey Leslie."

"I'm so sorry!" Leslie pouted and slammed into him for a hug.

"It's cool," he replied and pressed into the woman. She never gave him time of day before today so he made the most of it. He rubbed her back, rocked and grinded while she sobbed.

"Huh?" Leslie shrieked, suddenly alerted and pulled her face back enough to look at him. She blinked in disbelief but sure enough his rock hard erection throbbed between them. "Ewwww!"

"You know you like it..." Carlos mumbled at her back as she rushed away. The casket was finally lowered and the mourners lined up to toss dirt on it so they could go back to the rest of their lives.

Lives that would eventually lead here as well. Until then they would live it to the fullest.The boys in the hood were ready to go back to their comfort zones in the hood, now matter how dangerous it may be. Danger that made them live for the moment since tomorrow isn't promised. They would smoke, drink, fuck and pursue pleasures until it was their turn to be lowered into a box.

"I'm going with mom," Tara told her husband since Denise had a grieving sister to tend to. Val was wide eyed like a zombie at the second loss of her daughter. The streets had claimed her soul before they took her life

."I'll see you back at the room then," he agreed and gripped her booty while planting a kiss on her puckered lips.

"Come straight back to the room, Mister. I know you like these Virginia girls..." she teased.

"Nah, I love this Virginia girl!" he corrected and gave her another kiss. They both knew they could do this for hours and deliberately pulled away. Buddha watched her until she joined his mother and helped aunt Val to the car.

"You good B?" Rip asked as he came over. He sent Jeanine off to spend some time with her mother since she was heading up top with him when he left. Joey saw them come together and came over as well.

"Nah," Buddha assured him. "The fuck happened yo?"

"Ion know yet, but I'm going to find out," Rip vowed. This was business and personal since Ace was part of the Buddha crew and Kita was family.

"What about that nigga he put in the dirt?" Joey wondered since he remembered the problem with the hold out Kion.

"Nah, that was bruh people," Rip replied and nodded over to where Howard and Ace's family huddled. His face was a mask of confusion as he pondered this mystery. They weren't the only ones trying to decipher a mystery.

"Who are you?" G-money wondered as he zoomed in on Buddha through the binoculars. He noticed Buddha moved like a boss and the people around him deferred to him.He knew the who, what and where about Rip. He was supposed to be the boss but even he waited in a line to speak with Buddha before he left. He pulled his Cannon zoom lens up to his eye and snapped off a series of pictures. "Yeah, you definitely are somebody. I'll catch you later..."

*****

"New niggas..." Carlos said, shaking his head as he entered the motel parking lot. There was plenty of traffic by vehicle, foot and even a few bicycles. Proof that business was booming.

He had decimated the last crew that worked the hot hotel but the money was too good to stay vacant for long.That was good for Carlos since he had new players to set up for G-money to knock down. Plus, he got to keep the money he was making. Plus, there were new junky hoes milling about. The old ones either died, went to jail or rehab.

"New hoes!" he cheered for them as well. Both bros and hoes spotted his unique car and knew he came bearing gifts. The dealers could get coke at good prices and the prostitutes knew he spent well and bust quick which was a win/win in both worlds.

"Sup Los!" one of the young dealers greeted happily since he had just sold out. The night was young so he stood the chance to double up for the day.

"Cooling. I'ma catch up with y'all in a few..." he replied as he looked over him to overlook the hoes. Carlos was usually pro black except when it came to crack hoes. He insisted the white ones have more suction power in their jaws so he selected one and called her over.

"You tryna date?" she asked eagerly since she was trying to smoke.

"Nope! Tryna get my dick sucked!" he corrected and checked her over like a slave master picking a slave at market.

Which is sadly similar. He gripped her arm, leg and booty before checking her mouth. Crack addicts don't get regular dental care and sometimes have jagged edges from broken teeth. No one wants their dick scraped or cut so he checked her over. She checked out so he pulled her over to the office and got a room.

"You can fuck if you want," the woman shrugged since it didn't matter to her.

The younger dealers loved to fuck the white girls but Carlos was throat hound. He preferred to fuck faces when he got the chance. Can't make babies like that and he was too selfish to take care of any babies.

"Nope!" he laughed and whipped out the wood. The woman crawled over to him on the back and inhaled the dick.

'Gawk, gawk, gawk,' she gagged and slurped. She tugged and twisted her free hand until his legs began to shift. The pro-hoe knew what that meant and what to do. She clenched her jaws and dialed up the suction.

"Fuck!" Carlos shouted at the smoke stained ceiling and fed her some kiddie soup. He gripped her head to hold her in place as he skeeted down her throat.

"Check please!" the junkie joked. Junkies are known to have a good sense of humor. Makes sense though because if you're going to throw your life away you may as well have fun doing it.

"A little salad to go with your soup..." Carlos laughed and peeled her off a few green dollars from a larger stack of dollars. It was about to get even larger once he tucked his dick away. No sooner did he step back out the dealers pushed up in a rush.

"Sup bruh! Let me get something?" they pleaded with their cash out.

"A'ight, a'ight," he said with a big sigh like he was a big man. Truth be told these small time dealers wouldn't help keep that heavy nut sack off his face or G-money off his ass. He sold them the ounces and grams they would flip for their daily bread but he needed a bigger sacrifice. If not he had to serve Rip on a platter.

*****

"Leave me down here," Joey announced over the deafening silence at the table of the diner. Rip and Buddha needed to get back to their women but couldn't peel themselves out of the booth.

"Huh?" Buddha asked since the words sounded like just sounds amongst the clink of forks and spoons against plates and bowls.

"Yeah cuz, your cuz ain't moving right?" Rip asked since he couldn't put a finger on his feelings. He caught glimpses of Carlos during the funeral and noticed his odd behavior as well. The fall heat seemed to bother him more than the box containing his sibling.

"Nah, I..." Buddha began and shut back down. He remembered his role and conceded. "It's whatever you think is best B."

"Word," Rip nodded and accepted that he was now running the show. There was a time when he was content tricking off money and impregnating women while Buddha made them rich.

Now it was his turn.Not that he wasn't impregnating women since Jeanine was firmly knocked up. The difference was he was in the first committed relationship of his life. He felt honored that she chose him and would honor her decision with his loyalty. People bring a variety of things to the table but the best of them is loyalty. Looks fade, money spends, but loyalty is the lock.

"Yeah, we need one of us down here. Too much money at stake to risk with bruh," Joey reiterated. He was arguing on behalf of himself as well since being left down south with free reign meant he could go crazy. He was still skimming and scamming every chance he got and was getting rich.

"Say no more," Rip nodded and it was a done deal. A deal that would allow him to concentrate on running New York, since that was his ultimate goal. His close relationship with Giggles would now come in handy since he was at the wheel of the Camacho clan.

"Well, I'm out," Buddha sighed and stood. Rip beat him to his feet since he was just as eager to see his own woman. The men stepped outside and walked over to their cars.

"Yeah, you the boss B," G-money mocked as he watched through binoculars. Joey and Rip took turns dapping and hugging Buddha before each other. The deferment only confirmed his thoughts and nodded his head in agreement with himself.

He let the others pull off and pulled behind Buddha when he pulled out of the diner's parking lot. The relationship had already been confirmed so there was no surprise when he ended up at Val's home. He used the long lenses to capture shots of Buddha walking Tara back out to the rental car.

"You good babe?" Tara asked and rubbed Buddha's face as he pulled from the driveway.

"Nah," he admitted even if her stroke felt lovely on his cheek."Well, this might help..." she suggested rather suggestively and unbuckled her seat belt.

"What are you doing?" Buddha laughed as she made moves to do something she had never done before. Walking in on her mother so many times giving so many guys head had made her once vow to never suck a dick. This wasn't any dick though it was her husband's, so she leaned over and took him inside of her mouth.

"Ooooooh!" Tara had a lot to learn so the blow was more of an internship. She played around with his penis while he pretended like it was better than it was. He hummed and moaned like it felt better than it did since it's the thought that counts. At least the door was open and they had a lifetime to practice.

"We're here," he announced when they reached the hotel.

"Whew!" Tara said as if she had done work. She did manage to get him rock hard so he couldn't wait to get her inside of the room. He didn't even put his dick away when he got out of the car. "Baby!"

"Ain't nobody out here," he said when he came around and opened her door. He was almost right since he couldn't see the man taking pictures. Even if he paused since he wasn't trying to get pictures of anyone's dick.

The couple wasted no time once they got inside of the room. Pregnant pussy is the best pussy and he stayed rock hard just in anticipation. She peeled off her elastic pregnancy pants and positioned herself on the edge of the bed. This way Buddha could get it all without laying on the baby.

"Yup, yup!" Buddha said like a Teddy Riley song as he slid into that inferno she called a vagina. Tara alternated between winces and smiles as she watched her husband's face twist and contort in pleasure. She clamped that volcanic vice of a vagina tight when he made that face she knew all too well. "Fuck!"

"I know right," Tara laughed as he let loose the juice. If she wasn't already pregnant she might have gotten pregnant from the pent up tension spent inside of her. Buddha did the honors and went for the soapy washcloth. He washed them both before rejoining her in the bed. They scrambled under the covers and comforter and drifted off into sleep in each other's arms.

Chapter 2

"New Jersey pussy.." Bull said and shook his head when he returned to their spot in Newark.

He was relieved to see Donovan's car still out front but hoped he was finished with the cute little skeezer. Except he was about to find out the cute little skeezer was finished with him.

"Oh no!" Bull moaned when he walked in and saw the bloody mess left behind by the lovely little lunatic.

Donovan had that faraway gaze dead people have so there was no need to take his pulse. The only consolation was that he moved the money before the hit. It dawned on him on the way to his car that Queen wouldn't see it like that. She had plenty of money but only one son. Make that, none sons since Donovan was outta here.

"Fuck!" he shouted and pounded on the steering wheel. He got himself together and pulled away from the scene which was soon to be a crime scene.

Bull's mind raced a lot faster than his car did as he headed back over to New York city. He scrambled for excuses or explanations to offer Queen that could spare his life. He was paid to protect the prince but failed. He personally killed his predecessor who allowed Donovan to get robbed a few years back. No doubt there would be a price to pay for the dereliction of duty.

"Fuck!" Bull shouted when the car phone began to ring. Only two people had the number and he was pretty sure Donovan wasn't calling from the afterlife. It could only be Queen so he took the call.

"Where 'mi pickney? 'im not calling me back!" Queen wanted to know where her son was since he wasn't calling her back.

"Huh?" Bull replied quickly since he was a shooter, not a thinker and couldn't think of a lie as quickly as he could bust his gun.

"Donovan! Is 'im with you?" she barked.

"Oh, yeah. Nah, he um..." he stammered and stuttered.

"Is 'mi boy dead?" she had to wonder. These were pretty simple questions but he couldn't or wouldn't answer. Plus she knew her reckless son would join his father before she did.

"Who?" Bull asked and confirmed her suspicions.

"Come to 'mi 'ouse right now!" she demanded and hung up the phone.

"Fuck!" Bull cursed once more. No way was he just going to drive to his own death. Queens was right next to Brooklyn so he made his decision to swing the other direction. Pope hung out in a local pool hall used as his headquarters so that's where he went.

"Yo! That nigga Bull just pulled up out front!" a runner came running to report the intrusion.

"I'm about to wack that nigga right on the spot" El growled and stood to keep his word. He reached for a tech nine under the table but got called off.

14

"Chill son," Pope directed. He already got the news and knew what was going on. "Something tells me Mr Bull wants to switch teams."

"Huh?" El had to ask since he too was paid to shoot, not think. Plus he wasn't privy to the hit he just sent their way.

"Fall back!" Pope demanded since he understood demands better than directions. Most people do. They will huh? and what? until you scream at them. Then it's 'oh'.

"Hands up nigga!" one of Pope's men ordered as Bull stepped in. Bull didn't like taking orders from niggas but he disliked getting shot by niggas even more so he complied.

"A'ight B. I come in peace," he offered with his hands high.

"Peace, with a piece?" the searcher said when the search turned up a burner. He relieved Bull of his gun and gave him a shove towards the boss. Bull turned to lock in his face for a later date, if he lived past today's date.

"Sup Bull. What can I do for you?" Pope asked but answered before the man could open his mouth. "Let me guess. The young prince got whacked on your watch. Now you wanna jump ship?"

"And I know the stash spots, pick ups, lieutenants..." Bull added to add to his worth. Pope nodded since all those things were indeed worth their while in a war.

"So I guess you need a job? New place to lay your head?" Pope asked.

"Until this, is over," he replied, since he couldn't go home while Queen was still walking her fine ass on the surface of the earth.

"I got you bruh," Pope agreed and stood to shake the man's hand. He called over to another of his men and instructed. "Put son up in the hotel on Farmers. And give him his tool back."

"Boss..." El asked as he watched a dangerous opponent walk away without any bullet holes. After putting so many bullet holes in so many of their men over the years. "We really gonna rock with this sellout ass nigga? He supposed to ride or die but that nigga just cut and ran!"

"And we gonna work that nigga like a Hebrew slave!" Pope smiled. "He will sell out the whole crew! Then, and only then can you rock his ass to sleep!"

"Just say the word B," El snarled.

*****

"This the place," Blu confirmed when Queen's driver arrived at the Newark apartment.

"You sure?" she asked since Donovan's car was nowhere in sight. It was currently hosting a group of teens joyriding through the city since this was the car theft capital of the world.

"Yes ma'am. You want I should go in first?" he asked and reached for the door handle.

"No!" Queen shouted him down and pulled a pink nine millimeter from her purse. She hopped out of the car and stomped through the apartments like she owned the place. Her chunky jewelry attracted a group of local thugs but the gun swinging in her hand repelled them like mosquito spray.

"Ass fat tho!" one of the teens had to pronounce as she walked by. Queen turned at the disrespect and smiled.

"She on your tip B!" one of his friends declared and set off a round of high fives.

The door was still cracked when Queen arrived since the locals had got wind of the murder and relieved the dead man of stuff dead men don't need. No dead man had ever played a game of basketball so they peeled his Jordan's off his feet. Same for telling time, wearing jewelry or fancy jeans. He wouldn't need any of that shit so they took it all.

"Blood clot!" Queen moaned at her stripped down son stretched out on the floor. That's where he ended up after being robbed of anything worth robbing. She could see the hole in his chest where the super sharp stiletto ended his life.

The murder of her husband had just made her sad but this one was different. This one she pushed from her own womb. Something broke inside the woman, more than just her heart. She sat with her dead son and had a brief conversation.

"Mi responsible for dis. Should never got you into this game ya know," Queen nodded.

They certainly didn't need the money but she still allowed Donovan to follow in his father's footsteps. Now she would bury him right next to him in a Brooklyn graveyard. She planned to bury a lot of people right along with him. Even if it meant her own life since she now had nothing left to live for.

"See you soon mi youth," she purred and kissed his forehead. Then marched back out and shot the disrespectful teen in his forehead.

"Oh shit!" his friend shouted instead of running and got gunned down too. The others scattered and took shots in butts and backs until Queen's gun clicked empty.

"We gotta go!" Blu declared as he rushed over with his own gun out. The two guns would be nothing against all the guns sure to come out any second. He pulled his boss to the car while she still pointed and clicked the empty gun in every direction.

"Call di man dem!" Queen ordered and the driver picked up the car phone from the cradle.

"Who Queen?" he asked before she could reload her weapon since he didn't want to get shot too.

"Pope! Mi tink 'im behind this!" she nodded. Newark was a dangerous place and setting up shop was a dangerous prospect but still, she thought Pope was behind it. Her head kept nodding since they were engaged in an all out war for turf.

They were engaged in back to back shootings on the streets that were getting them nowhere. This was his Nagasaki and Hiroshima designed to break her back. The driver followed directions and called the pool hall. The phone was passed around a few times before the familiar baritone voice filled the car through the speaker.

"Is this the Queen?" Pope asked and did a curtsey she couldn't see. He motioned for the door and cleared his office so he could have some privacy.

"You kill 'mi pickney? You drop Donovan?" she asked calmly despite the rage bubbling in her soul.

"Huh? Someone killed my stepson?" he asked as he removed his dick from his slacks.

"Yeah, it was you," she declared. The smug tone told her he was behind the murder even if he didn't kill him himself.

"Slow down baby. Tell me what happened..." he asked while stroking himself erect. He often jacked off any time he got her on the line since her sexy voice drove him crazy. She knew it too since he would grunt loudly when he reached his peak. She wouldn't give him the satisfaction today.

"Oh, you'll read about it," she declared and hung up the phone.

"Shit!" Pope fussed at being cut short. He walked over to the door and looked around the pool hall. A group of around the way girls were dancing to LL's song by the same name. He called one over and pulled her inside the office.

"Ohh!" the teen shrieked when he bent her over his desk and snatched her jeans down. She gave her consent by arching her back even though he was going in with or without it. The tight, young box was better than nothing but he still wanted the Queen of Brooklyn. He pretended it was her bent over his desk and beat her back out.

"Shit! Argh!" Pope grunted as he bust inside the young girl. Her little boyfriend had seen her go into the office and could only pout when she limped out with a couple hundred dollars in her pocket. They would just go spend the money and pretend it didn't happen since this was Pope's world at the moment.

Sa'id Salaam

Chapter 3

"Twenty thousand dollars..." Giggles fussed as he paced the living room floor.

"Is nothing papi!" Rosalinda reminded as she rocked their new baby. He now had more kids with her than his own. There would most likely be more since he practically moved into the downtown high rise with her. He rarely got out to the island to see Jennifer and her two kids. Only one of which belonged to him even though he still didn't know it. "Drop in the bucket baby."

"How about I drop this in your bucket..." Giggles giggled and grabbed his dick.

"Don't threaten me with a good time!" she shot back and began to pull her dress up.

"When I get back," he laughed and shook his head. Rosalinda was down for the get down at the drop of a dime.

So was his wife at home but she reminded him too much of her father. Plus he planned to kill her mother as soon as he figured out how to get to the millions she had tucked away. Then he could do what Miguel should have done and retire.

Turn the show over to the next clown and enjoy the fruits of his labor. Not only did he get to wear the crown he would get to live to talk about it. The best lessons in life are history lessons since history was sure to repeat itself. The last few kings of New York all died on the throne. He would be the one to retire with the crown on his head.

"Ok papi. Ju know it's jour pussy! Anytime ju want it!" she mocked his wife and snickered. Giggles just smirked and shook his head on the way out.

"Sup unc," Poncho greeted when Giggles stepped from the building.

"You," he greeted in return and dapped him up. Poncho had pulled Giggles car around but hopped in the passenger seat since the man still liked to drive himself. He muttered and cursed to himself all the way uptown to meet the crooked cops.

They made their point about being punctual when they doubled their fee. Giggles would play along until he figured out a way to get rid of them. Killing cops came with lots of problems and he already had enough of those. His assistance to Queen may have gotten him the throne but it was costing him money since both sides were too busy killing each other instead of selling coke. He would make up for it by selling guns to both sides of the battle.

"Those cops again?" Poncho asked when they reached the same restaurant as the first meet. Giggles whipped his head in the kid's direction when he heard the tremble of fear.

"Si," he nodded but couldn't help but wonder if officer Hall wasn't right about him. Would he give up the goods if pressed? He couldn't be sure but damn sure knew he needed to know.

"Here comes our favorite drug lord," William laughed when he saw Giggles park in front.

"Your favorite. My money is on the Queen. That bitch is ruthless," she cheered. "And got a fat ass!"

"Ass is fat," her partner had to agree. He wasn't sure how a fat ass would help in the ongoing turf war but still had to give credit where due.

"Comé esta?" Giggles announced when he reached the table and the cops continued their conversation as if he wasn't there. Williams looked at the Frank Mueller watch on his wrist to make sure he was on time before speaking.

"Well hello there Mr Giggles!" he greeted happily since the man was actually a few minutes early. The cops had been a half hour early to make sure no one ever got the drop on them.

"Not sure if you can say Mr, Giggles?" Hall asked and twisted her full lips.

"Right! Miss Giggles, sounds like a stripper," William laughed. Giggles couldn't wipe the perpetual smile off his face even though he was seething. What neither cop knew was that they were dealing with a certified psychopath. And if they kept playing with him he would throw it all away and splatter them both right there in the booth.

"Take it easy there Giggles," Regina smiled when she saw smoke billowing from his ears. "Just busting your chops like we used to do Miguel!"

"He could take a joke," Williams laughed but looked at the uniform cops they always posted since Miguel actually couldn't take a joke. The cops were there for their security.

"Si," Giggles nodded and sat. He sat the bag of cash down at his feet and looked back and forth between the two cops.

"I need something for my money," he began, since he was paying twice as much for the same services Miguel received. He may as well get his money's worth.

"But of course!" Williams agreed. He was ready to shake down rivals and renegades. Or arresting any competition whether they had drugs, guns or not. They kept extra of each in the trunk to make charges stick on anyone.

"Check..." Giggles replied and filled them in while looking at Poncho seated in the car.

"Not a bad idea," Regina had to admit once Giggles had stood and walked away. They had their orders and he had appointments in both Brooklyn and Queens.

*****

"What's this place?" Poncho asked when Giggles pulled into a Brooklyn driveway. It was a good question since the last person he brought here was murdered, dismembered and fed to dogs.

"Grab that bag," he replied for an answer.

"Which one?" the kid asked since there were two. They were identical but he still wanted to be sure.

"The one of the left," Giggles replied to make it easier on the kid. Even though it didn't since Poncho wasn't sure if Giggles meant his right or the kids. He made a decision and grabbed the one on his right since it was his left.

"Fuck!" Poncho grunted when the weight of the bag nearly dropped him to the ground. He wouldn't punk out so he mustered everything he had in him and managed to get it to the door just as it was pulled open.

"Queen!" Giggles announced when he saw the woman open the door.

"Yes. I'm handling things personally!" she declared since this was personal. A nod sent a large man who rushed over and took the bag from Poncho. The kid used his back, legs and chest but the man grabbed it with one hand and brought it inside.

"I'm sorry to hear about Donovan. That was my guy!" Giggles proclaimed. That part was true since he actually liked the man. Especially after Donovan crossed Miguel and spared his life.

"Which is why I need you. What did you bring us?" she asked and turned her attention to the bag.

"Everything you need to end this shit!" Giggles snarled and pulled back the zipper. The large man looked on and smiled when the Uzis began coming out of the bag. Next came the extended clips and boxes of bullets. "Last but not least..."

"Bumba clot!" Queen cheered when he produced a grenade.

"I could only get my hands on one," he offered almost apologetically.

"He is one man!" she said and stuck her chest out. It had the opposite effect since she had some really, really nice breasts.

"Well, handle this shit so we can get back to business!" Giggles ordered them to remind them that he ran New York. He turned on his heels and headed for the door. Poncho was right behind him and they got back into the car.

Neither said a word as they bent corners and cruised streets. Giggles spun a u-turn in the street to park in front of a pool hall on the other side. Poncho could hear the guys repeating Giggles name before they even opened the door. A moment later El appeared at the door with a welcoming smile.

"Grab that bag," Giggles ordered as he stepped out. He moved through the men like a politician as the kid struggled with the bag once again. Once again he was helped out since El stepped up.

"I'll take that for you lil man," El said when he saw Poncho struggling with the bag. He let out a slight grunt since it was heavier than he expected.

"My man Giggles!" Pope cheered as he came out of his office to meet the boss.

"Pope," he replied and dapped the man up. Once the pleasantries were out of the way he got right down to business. "Are you still in control of Queens, or do I need to send my people out here? Because all I'm hearing about is shootouts!"

"I have this under control!" Pope assured him. "We just need more firepower!"

"And you have it," Giggles replied and pulled the zipper once again.

"Yooooo!" El cheered and actually clapped his hands when the Uzis started coming out.Meanwhile Poncho just blinked as the exact number of guns, bullets and clips came out of this bag just like the one at Queens. He could only blink some more when a grenade came out last like last time.

"I could only get my hands on one," Giggles offered unapologetically. "So make it count!"

"Oh, I'm gonna make it count alright..." Pope said like a man with a plan. Not to mention a little help from a lunatic.

*****

"I need you to make a run," Giggles announced when they reached the block.

"Me?" Poncho cheered eagerly. Riding with the boss was one thing but making moves for the boss was something else.

"Go see Sam in Chelsey. Grab that," he directed and passed off the keys.

"Grab that," he repeated and nodded. He was still nodding and repeating as he pulled off the block and headed downtown.

He only made it a few blocks down Fifth avenue before flashing lights killed his vibe. He checked his speed against the posted signs and knew he wasn't speeding. Nor was he smoking so he turned the radio down and pulled over. The cops didn't bother running the plates since they knew who the car belonged to. Instead they hopped out and took both sides with hands on their guns.

"Driver's license and registration," the cop on the driver's side ordered while the other shone his flashlight into the backseat.

"Ion know where, I'm just..." Poncho stammered since he didn't have a license and had no idea where the registration was. He remembered from movies people getting papers from the glove box so he reached over and pulled open.

"Gun!" the other cop announced when a pistol fell from the glove box. He pulled his own gun and aimed it at the kid's head.

"Don't do it!" the other shouted and yanked his own weapon when Poncho began to reach for the weapon.

"My bad, I..." he was saying before getting snatched from the car and quickly cuffed. The cop pressed him against the car with his hands secured behind his back. That allowed his partner to holster his weapon and search the car.

"Jackpot!" he chuckled when the glove box also gave up a fresh brick of cocaine.

"A gun and drugs?" the cop holding Poncho asked in his ear. "You're going to prison for a long time kid!"

"Huh? Me? Por que?" Poncho pleaded and had to pee all of a sudden.

"Yes, you!" the second cop replied, then explained the why, "Because you have drugs and a gun!"

"It's not mine! I..." Poncho pleaded. Both cops looked at each, then back to the kid to let him finish.

"Whose car is it! Whose drugs?" one asked.   "If it's not yours then whose is it?"

"Giggles! I work for him! I am going to see Sam in Chelsey. To grab that..." he explained even if he still didn't know what that was supposed to be.

"I see," the second cop sighed as the first one uncuffed the kid. Poncho rubbed his wrist since the cuffs left a mark. He stopped when the cop handed him the pistol back.

"Thanks I..." Poncho was saying but wouldn't reach said.

"Gun!" the other cop shouted and lifted his to Poncho's chest. A couple quick tugs on the trigger knocked chucks in his chest and out his back. Poncho slammed against the car and slid down to the ground. His eyes were open but he didn't see when Williams and Hall pulled up to make their report.

"Pay up!" Regina demanded since she won the bet.

"Yeah, yeah..." Williams said, twisting his lips.

He put his hundred that the kid would at least make it to the precinct before snitching. She bet he wouldn't make it to the backseat of the police car before giving up the goods. The beat cops tucked the kilo of coke as payment and wrote up the report of the kid pulling a gun on them. It would be ruled a good shooting but even better since Giggles eliminated a future problem.

Sa'id Salaam

Chapter 4

"You ok?" Tara asked when she heard Buddha let out a sigh as the plane skidded on the runway at LaGuardia airport. Despite the occasion, Virginia was a break from the stress of Highbridge. Even though Buddha fell back from daily operations he was still called upon and counted on for input.

"Huh? Yeah!" he replied since he was looking forward to going back to school. High school was fun on several levels since he played ball, fucked cheerleaders and sold weed. But college stimulated his mind in every subject.

Especially the business classes that confirmed and refined some of the things he was already practicing in the streets.His favorite was diversity. He had plans to legitimize the stacks of cash Rip turned in every week. Business was booming with new avenues opening every day. Rip doubled the re-up once again and on the verge of doing it again. It was all going so well Buddha knew it wouldn't last. It couldn't last because life just doesn't work like that.

"Well, Keisha just beeped," Tara announced. They would stop at the first payphone they found to answer the pages they received during the flight since Buddha didn't drive to the airport.

"Word," he replied since he had received one from Trouble along with the 9-11 code. Buddha didn't think much of the emergency code since Trouble used it for everything from how much baking soda to use while cooking coke to asking about a bump on his back. They both used the phone and got the same news.

"Keisha is in labor!" Tara cheered and he knew they were going straight to the hospital. Trouble reported the same and specified which hospital. They caught a cab to Columbia Presbyterian since they chose to start the new life in the same place that gave Buddha a new lease on his life.

"I know," Buddha laughed after getting the same report from a frantic Trouble. They collected their baggage and made a beeline to the hospital.

"Sup yo!" Trouble greeted and hugged his mentor when he walked into the hospital. The maternity ward was upstairs but this was as far as he got.

"I'm going up..." Tara said as she passed and went up to the maternity ward. She spotted an older version of Black Keisha and knew right away who she was. "You must be Keisha's mom?"

"I am?" she asked back to find out who she was. Especially since Tanika and Chrissy were nowhere to be found. Keisha had abandoned her old friends in favor of her new love so it wasn't their fault they didn't get the message.

"I'm Tara. I..." Tara began and paused since she wasn't sure what exactly she was. She was the boss's wife who wasn't technically the boss any more.

"Oh! Ok, my baby told me all about you!" the woman cheered and wrapped her into a hug. Tara wasn't sure why the love until the woman explained. "She told me you encouraged her to stay in school! Now she wanna go to college just like you!"

"She told you about me?" Tara beamed proudly. Being the child of a crackhead didn't give her much to mentor anyone about, until now.

"Did she!" the woman reeled and laughed. "Tara this, Tara said, Tara taught me! I can't thank you enough!"

"You just did!" Tara assured her and initiated the next hug. This one was cut short when a nurse came out with news of a baby boy. "Hey, I'm an auntie!"

"Oh Lord, I'm a grandmother!" her mother moaned. She ran her hands over her fine frame as they headed in to meet the newest member of the Buddha crew. "Still fine tho!"

Meanwhile, young Trouble was a mess downstairs. He wasn't sure if he needed to throw up or pass out. Part of him wanted to run and never look back but the other part knew he was where he was supposed to be.

"Breathe B!" Buddha urged to calm the kid.

"Yo, I'm 'bout to be a whole pops out this bitch son!" he marveled at the prospect. Little did he know he already was since Kareem Trouble Green had just made his grand entrance into the world.

"Word B," Buddha sighed since Tara was due in a few more months herself.

Feeling that baby moving inside of her was a life changing experience. He just didn't know how he was supposed to change it. He was a hood nigga to his heart and only felt comfortable in his own hood. Highbridge was loud, dirty and dangerous but it was all he knew.

"You should fall back from the block," Buddha finally verbalized. He had thought about it a hundred times before but even more after E-baby got out. He and Monte were now just regular guys and he loved that for them. Even if he didn't think he could ever get all the way out.

"And do what?" Trouble asked and looked up at Buddha for an answer. All he knew was the streets, so what else could he do with himself.

Not to mention he was good at it. Trouble spent his days cooking coke, supplying the spots and reconciling the books. He was an Amazon hub all by himself. Buddha ran through a variety of answers in his mind but not one of them made it to his mouth. Because they were his thoughts and he couldn't, wouldn't impose them on the kid.

"College," Buddha said just above a mumble since he knew the kid wasn't the scholastic type. He definitely had the brains but school is more than brains. Hard work can often make up for what anyone lacks in brains.

"Mr Green?" a nurse asked when she came looking for Trouble."

"Oh shit," he replied and felt his knees buckle.

"I bet," Buddha laughed and kept him from falling. He was too shook to answer so Buddha answered for him. "Here yo!"

"Yeah, that's you!" the woman said since she remembered when he brought Keisha in the taxi. She noticed him turning green in his face but didn't get paid to sugarcoat shit. "Nah son, you should have thought about this when you were pushing in, instead of pulling out! Now it's time to man up!"

"Word!" Buddha seconded but part of it was for himself. He would have to man up as well since he was right behind him on the daddy list. A long list and Rip was way ahead. Not to mention Jeanine was pregnant too. Somehow this one was different from the other ones since she was almost always by his side.

"Word!" Trouble agreed as well. He stuck that bird chest out and followed the nurse up to meet his name sake.

*****

"Thanks uncle Rip!" Trouble cheered at the diaper hack Rip showed the new parents.

"How you learn to change diapers like that?" Keisha wanted to know.

"Shit, he got like twelve kids!" Trouble laughed at the exaggeration.

"Nine nigga," he shot back and turned to Keisha to answer her question. "Ma dukes taught me that with my little brother."

"Word," Keisha nodded as she swaddled the baby to take him home. Trouble wanted them both to stay with him until she reminded him that he cooked coke in the apartment every day. She still brought the baby by when she took him out in the fancy ass stroller Trouble bought.

"I'll be through later, when I wrap up around here," he said and leaned in for a kiss. It was supposed to be a peck on the lips but once again turned into a tongue wrestling affair with a handful of ass in his palms.

"Yeah, that's good to have them back to back so they can grow up together!" Rip suggested and broke off the kiss quicker than if had thrown ice water on the couple.

"No time soon!" Keisha winced and squeezed her legs tight. It was too close to pushing a whole baby out of her to be talking about doing it again. This kiss was just a peck and she strolled the baby out in his chariot.

"Err thing good?" Rip asked once they were alone. Keisha may have been around all day but they still never talked shop in front of her.

"Hell yeah!" Trouble cheered and got specific. "Bout to hit the projects off with their pack. Just took care of the playground and 170th. Joey is supposed to be here in a few."

"Make sure his is raw, because..." Rip was saying but the kid already knew.

"Cuz its way less time getting caught with coke than crack!" he repeated verbatim from hearing it so many times. Not that it explained the why since that shit was like getting in more trouble for applesauce than plain old apples. "Why tho?"

"Cuz, niggas fuck with the crack while white people just do coke. So they are shooting at us, tryna spare them," he snarled at the ridiculous drug laws.

"Damn!" Trouble said and shook his head. "Anyway, after Delilah comes through we're gonna be mad low B!"

"I'm going to spit at Giggles ndem in a few," Rip said and looked at his watch.

"Hole up, I'll ride with you!" the kid cheered since he loved to go along to the re-up.

"Not this time yo," Rip replied since Giggles told him to come alone. He had to run through his latest activities to make sure he wasn't in any trouble. Most of the troubles in his life had a vagina but Jeanine was the only chick he was hitting at the moment so he was good.

"Oh, ok," the kid said and twisted his lips ruefully since he wanted to go. There was plenty left to do around there so he dapped Rip up and got busy.

The first order of business was getting everyone their re-up. Joey was moving twenty bricks every week in Richmond but word was starting to spread so he was coming every few days. The Staten Island crew was up to ten a week since Delilah stepped up. Sampson was too busy clubbing and fucking to focus on business.

Then he had to cook a mountain of crack to feed the voracious appetite of the Burroughs's crack addicts. Each spot was running through a kilo of cooked coke every day. Plus the growing market of bougie chicks and pretty boys who preferred to sniff their coke with manicured fingernails of fancy spoons.

He donned his gloves and respirator so he could get down to business. Halfway through the first batch Josh came through to help with the chopping and packaging. They listen to rappers rapping about the life they really lived every day.

"That's gotta be Joey?" Trouble guessed when they heard the doorbell ring.

"I got it," Josh said since he didn't budge. Trouble was becoming a boss so he didn't do certain things when other people were around to do them. Just like Buddha and Rip did with him.

"Sup yo," Joey greeted when the door was pulled open for him. His face reacted to the freshly cooked crack smell in the air.   "Smells like I'm right on time!"

"What up tho," Trouble replied and dapped him up. "You been by to see papi on Jerome?"

"Nigga I ain't new to this!" Joey shot back. Of course he had been by the shop to swap out delivery vehicles.

New Yorkers got knocked every week transporting drugs to the lucrative southern markets because they weren't careful. He was though which is why he used different vehicles and always traveled during rush hours to blend in with traffic. He never made round trip trips in the same vehicle since they installed license plate readers on the bridges. Even still, he was looking for a better way to move drugs south.

"Word," Trouble replied and headed down the hall to collect his work. Twenty kilos is less than fifty pounds but worth over a million once it was broken down into its smallest increments. He exchanged it for the four hundred thousand dollars Joey had brought up.

Trouble returned with the bag and saw the stacks of bills Joey was placing on the table. He retrieved the counter from under the table and began running the bills through it. Joey twisted his lips like he was being tried but he kept them closed since this was Rip's rule. All receipts counted and accounted for every day. He was oddly more effective than Buddha in some ways, while still totally reckless in others.

"Check," Joey announced and twisted his lips like a Flava Flav 'yeah boyeee!' when the count counted up to what it was supposed to count up to. Trouble didn't respond since he wouldn't cheer for someone doing what they were supposed to do. That would be like a man wanting props for taking care of his own kids, cuz that's what they are supposed to do anyway.

"Be safe yo," Trouble said and dapped him up.

"Word B," he smiled down at the kid and remembered why they all liked him so much. He looked over to Josh stuffing crack into vials and shouted, "A'ight yo!"

"Peace!" Josh said back as he headed out the door.Joey had already made his rounds around the building and borough so he loaded up and got on the road. The coke was safely tucked away in a false gas tank devised by Puerto

Rican papi. It was close enough to the real tank to throw off the dogs from the smell of gas.

"Let's get it!" he pumped himself up as he made the trek that could take five hours or ten years in the feds.

Five hours later he pulled into the apartments and the real work began. The customers were all waiting for his call but he had things to do before he could call. Taking out ten percent of the pure coke and replacing it with cut was a lot of work. Work that would net him two extra keys of pure coke but he cut them too. Now he had a few ounces of pure coke to snort with his Richmond strippers and an extra two kilos to sell to pad his pockets.

Sa'id Salaam

Chapter 5

"Oye!" was called out when Rip turned onto the Camacho block. Miguel Camacho may have been dead and buried but it would always be known as the Camacho block. It was still the Camacho clan except now it was Giggles posted up on the stoop with a detail of security, cronies and yes men all around him.

"Fuck!" Rip declared and winced when he saw the tan ass cheeks bouncing under a pair of tiny shorts. His eyes went wide when he saw they belonged to Rosalinda. She had bounced back quite nicely after childbirth. The eyes went wider when she went and sat between Giggles' legs like he was his woman.

"Sup yo," Rip greeted when he got out. He greeted and dapped his way up the block until he reached the boss.

"Hola hermano!" Giggles greeted loud enough to let everyone around know he considered this boricua from the Bronx as a brother. He never called any of them that, even the late Poncho.

"Hola hermano," he replied as the boss shooed his woman so he could stand. Then hug the man. Rip saw a mural of Poncho was painted on the wall of the building he had lived in when he was alive, before the cops un-alived him.

"Sorry to hear about little man B," Rip offered. He sounded genuine even though he didn't give a fuck. This was New York and niggas get shot every day B.

"Yeah," Giggles said with a shrug and was done with it just as quickly. He didn't tell anyone about the test the kid failed that got him put on a mural. It was his secret even if he wanted to pee on the mural if he got the chance. "Come inside..."

"Si," he replied and followed him inside the building. Rip wondered what was up since no one else followed them inside. He was here to collect over a hundred pounds of cocaine so someone usually carried it to the car for him. As soon as they reached the empty apartment he asked, "Que pasa?"

"I want you to join the family is what's up," Giggles offered plainly. He isolated the man to ask just in case he got turned down. He would accept it from Rip even if he didn't want it witnessed.

"You know I run the Buddha crew B! I'm boss now," he said as his chest puffed out on its own.

"I know. You still can, just with us. Like a franchise. Same as always," he explained. It made sense since they had been working closely for years.

"Franchise huh?" Rip nodded as the thought rolled around in his head. It was the same word Buddha used when Miguel was alive. "Franchisees get better prices..."

"The best!" Giggles confirmed and sealed the deal with a pound and a hug. With that done he moved on to the next part of the plan. "I need you to make a run with me?"

"Sure," Rip agreed without asking when or where.

"Good! You been to Cali?" Giggles asked but didn't wait for a reply before continuing. "We're going to meet the connect!"

*****

"Cali? Word?" Buddha reeled when Rip relayed his plans. He liked the idea of being a franchise but meeting the connect was even better. He and Miguel were moving towards that direction anyway. It would mean better prices and more muscle. "When?"

"Today!" Rip sighed since Jeanine had just come up. He took her everywhere he went but wouldn't be taking her on this trip.

"Do that shit B!" his partner encouraged and gave him a pound.

"I am. Now I gotta break the news to my girl," he sighed.

"Your what?" Buddha asked. He heard him just fine but just never heard him call any chick by that title before.

"Word," he laughed and headed across the hall. He was relieved to see the rest of the family was out on some family outing so he could get his point across. That's why he started undressing as soon as he walked into the apartment.

"Um, what are you doing?" Jeanine asked with a giggle since she knew. Her vagina gave a happy quiver since it knew what time it was. A field trip to pound town.

"About to wax that ass one time!" Rip laughed and she began slipping out of her clothes as well. She flipped over and tooted the booty up so they could work around her baby bump.

Rip planted kisses on her back and backside as he fondled her box from behind. It only took a few seconds to turn the box into a juice box and soak his fingers. He got caught up running his fingers in and out to her melody of moans, then replaced them with the dick.

"Aye papi!" Jeanine hissed and Rip twisted his lips since they heard Alva moaning that this morning when Monte got his morning backshots.

"He would happily deal with it since it was certainly a lot better than when she was a base head.He looked down and watched the slow motion porno show as he slid in and out. It wasn't long until she coated his dick with that good, creamy lotion. The pussy just got better and wetter with every stroke until she shuddered from a strong orgasm. He wasn't that far behind her and filled her up with the siblings who wouldn't make it.

"Now, what's on your mind?" Jeanine asked when he finally got himself together.

"Huh? Who?" Rip asked but his woman just twisted her lips like, 'yeah right'. He couldn't help but to laugh and love the way she knew him so well.

"You nigga! Err time you want something you lay down some good pipe first," she reminded. "Now, let's hear it."

"Ok, first of all. I lay down some good pipe err time regardless," he corrected. "And yeah, I gotta make a run out to Cali. Business."

"Oh..." Jeanine pouted and rubbed her belly. She did that whenever stressed since the life inside always brought her comfort.

"Business ma!" he vowed and crossed his heart.

"Oh, I get it," she shrugged and sighed. His business was good for her business since she still had chicks slinging coke in the clubs back home.

"But..." Rip asked since he knew his woman pretty well as well. Jeanine wasn't one of those combative chicks who always complained. A simple pout could usually get her point across.

"I'm just saying, I've been to Cali before. When I was on my stud shit, and them Cali hoes something else!" she declared and closed her eyes like she could still taste it. "You ever had some California pussy yo?"

"You know who you sound like right now?" he laughed but she didn't. "A-yo ma. Word is bond I'm not touching no broads out there B! Just business!"

"Now see! Don't vow! Don't put that on your word!" Jeanine pleaded. "Because if you break it, I won't be able to trust you! And I need to be able to trust you! You're going to be my baby daddy! All my babies daddy! Every last one of them! I need your word to be good!"

"My word is my bond!" Rip declared and puffed out his chest. He was twenty one now and hadn't broken it yet.

"I know," she purred and kissed his lips. "You have my permission to get your dick sucked. You ever had some California head B?"

"You stupid yo!" he cracked up. "Swear I love your ass!"

The room went silent as the heavy words descended from the ceiling. The couple was clearly a couple and knew they loved each other since they spent every possible second together. Even when in separate cities they closed the gap by talking on the phone several times a day and night. For all the emotions and actions they never said it, until now.

"Word B! I love you too papi," Jeanine said. She meant it so much it pushed a tear from her eye. They shared a moment and a hug before he had to pack a bag and head back over to Harlem.

*****

"Rich nigga shit!" Giggles declared when the driver pulled up to a private hangar at JFK. He was right too because rich niggas from every race were here to use their private jets.

"Word!" Rip agreed and watched a Chinese nigga board a jet with two bad chicks of his arm. He and Giggles were flying solo except for a few duffle bags filled with a few million dollars in them. It was his first time flying private but vowed it wouldn't be his last. In the interim he had a pressing question. Once the plane lifted off he decided to ask. "Why are you taking me yo?"

"Because," Giggles replied and contemplated on how forthcoming he wanted to be. He had already placed this much trust in the man so he continued. "I trust you. You don't want to be king."

"Nah, I just like money," Rip admitted. Being acting boss of the Buddha crew was more than enough for him. Running the city was once Buddha's goal but he just liked the money. That's the down side to the crown. That mother fucker gets heavy.

"Too many people in the family want the throne. You have to kill the king to be the king," he put out and watched Rip as he processed the statement. It took a few seconds before his eyes went wide with understanding. He now knew Giggles killed Miguel. Which meant he killed Javier too since he had never been seen again.

"Word?" he reeled as he reflected back on the funeral. He vividly recalled how Giggles acted like it was more of a cookout than a funeral. Oddly it suddenly reminded him of the most recent funeral he attended. Carlos was preoccupied and didn't shed a tear, just like Giggles.

"Word! He was a dinosaur. Didn't want to move with the times," he justified. "That's why I trust someone from outside the family over any of them."

"Word," Rip repeated even if he didn't feel it. He trusted Buddha over everyone including his own mother, baby mothers and the rest of creation.

"I trust you tho hermano. You will be my right hand man!" Giggles cheered and held out his hand. Rip took that hand and squeezed his allegiance.

Giggles fired up a blunt and popped a bottle once they reached cruising altitude. They were both soon higher than the jet so Rip laid back and looked at life speeding through the window. Six hours later they were landing in LA.

"Rich nigga shit!" Rip repeated when he saw the limo pull right into the hangar to collect him and Giggles. The driver loaded the duffle bags into the trunk and pulled away.

"You ain't seen nothing yet!" Giggles assured him and he was right. The mountain views were spectacular but nothing compared to the mansions that overlooked them. The driver acted like a tour guide as he pointed out the various houses of the rich and famous. He said nothing when they arrived at the house of the rich and infamous.

"Fuck!" Rip announced at the gated mansion with a fountain in the middle of a circular driveway. Five exotic cars totalled two million dollars parked out front. Huge doors opened and a small man walked out and threw his arms as wide as his smile.

"My man Giggles!" the host who owned the most cheered.

"Don Chavez!" he cheered, cheesed and took him up on the hug. "This is the guy I tell you about."

"Mr rest in peace," Don Chavez cheered and hugged Rip too. It had been so long since Gabriel had adopted the nickname he almost forgot that was what it actually meant. He was called Rip long before he ever bust his gun and made someone rest in peace.

"Nice to meet you," he replied in the hug."I hear a lot about you?" Don Chavez asked like it was a test. Because it was.

"I haven't heard anything about you," he replied and passed on behalf of himself and Giggles.

"Si, si. Muy bueno!" he laughed and escorted them inside. A full blown party was happening out by the pool as they passed by. Rip looked at the topless women frolicking in the water and shook his head.

They arrived in the den where a wall of televisions played several soccer games from all over the globe. Don Chavez sat in a large, throne-like chair and motioned for his guest to sit on the sofa across from him. A pretty maid served drinks, smiles and cleavage before leaving them alone to talk.

"So, Giggles tells me you are a good earner?" Don Chavez asked, looking towards Giggles who nodded in confirmation. Rip wanted to share the credit with his partner but decided against it. Sometimes it good to shut the fuck up, this was one of them so he kept his speech to a minimum.

"Si," he agreed and waited for the rest since he still wasn't sure why he was here.

"Good. Muy bueno! Very good!" the man laughed.

"We need you to handle the re-up from now on," Giggles finally explained. "Like I said, I don't trust no one in the family but you. And I can't fly out here every week and Run New York."

"Word," Rip agreed while putting it together in his head. Joey was running Virginia just fine and Trouble handled the Bronx. Both men watched as the wheels turned in his head. Don Chavez was a master so he knew just when to skeet a little grease to make the wheels turn smoother.

"Of course you will be compensated handsomely for your efforts. One hundred thousand a trip," he offered.

"Plus, your bricks go down to ten Gs each," Giggles added and sealed the deal."Run it!" Rip agreed. This just doubled or tripled his worth just that quickly.

"This of course requires the utmost discretion?" The plug asked to make sure he knew the answer. Another test and Rip quickly passed it as well.

"But of course!" he shot back adamantly.

"Can't even tell your closest friend!" Giggles insisted since he knew how close he and Buddha were.

"You already know tho!" he shot back since sometimes you have to cheat on a test. Giggles smiled and nodded at the answer.

"It's settled then!" Don Chavez cheered and lifted his drink. They all lifted theirs and clinked them in the air before tossing them back. "Now, what's this nasty business in New York! Brooklyn and Queens?"

"Turf war," Giggles shrugged like he wasn't in the middle of it. Rip knew it was a lie since Giggles had giggled about how he was playing both sides on the flight. He knew that was a no-no but the plug reiterated it.

"Stay out of it! It's bad for business!" Don demanded sternly, then switched gears. "Now, go out by the pool and pick you a girl. Or two!"

"Two!" Giggles laughed since he regularly cheated on his side piece and wife.

"Word..." Rip sighed and remembered his word. He also remembered Jeanine's allowance so he picked a busty Asian girl and got himself some good Asian head.

Chapter 6

"Word? Wow! Damn! Son!" Buddha reeled when Rip filled him in on the trip. He had no desire to get back in the game but wouldn't have minded taking a private jet out to Cali. Even without some Cali head.

He agreed with the move and also the instructions not to speak about it to anyone. Anyone else but him since they were close enough to almost be the same person. So close Rip had to run it by his best friend for a second opinion. If the plane ever got popped he was looking at a couple decades in a federal prison. If it didn't he was looking at millions of more dollars.

"An extra hundred grand a week!" he said and shook his head.

"That's you B! But we still getting them things for ten Gs! Son!" Buddha declared. Rip was ready to cut him in on his cut but Buddha wouldn't hear of it. He was the one risking it all on a plane filled with drugs or cash.

"Word," Rip relented. He had something else on his mind so he put it out there as well. "Jeanine found a house yo."

"Buy it!" Buddha immediately shot back. One thing he was sure of was real estate. It and cocaine were the best money makers in America. They were almost finished renovating their first building and he was already looking for more.

"It's in Virginia tho," he sighed. Just that quickly he had picked up on and adapted Don Chavez's habit of asking questions without actually asking.

"Still get it B! All this cash is worthless unless we do something with it!" he shot back like a business major. He and Tara were spreading his money around into different ventures and venues. Buddha was smart enough to see the business in everything he saw. He had just bought ice cream for the entire block and realized how much money they generated. Now he was researching buying trucks of his own.

"You right," Rip agreed. There was only one thing left to share so he saved it for last. "You ever had some Asian head my nigga?"

"Yeah, have you?" Tara asked as she caught the tail end of the question when she walked in.

"Ion even know what that means..." Buddha replied and lifted his chin.

"Sup ma," Rip greeted and hugged his sister in law.

"Hey there Mr Rip. Where's Jeanine?" she asked.

"With my moms. She's going back to Virginia later tonight," he replied on his way out and back across the hall. The two friends dapped, hugged and departed.

"Speaking of head..." Buddha dared once they were alone.

"Mmhm," she hummed and twisted her lips. She untwisted them a moment later since you can't give head like that.

*****

"Awe man!" Trouble groaned at what could be trouble.

"What?" Keisha wondered since she knew that tone. He was counting money while she fed their son but didn't like the final tally.

"Huh? Oh, nah. Nothing. Err thing is good," he lied but she knew it. You can't spend that much time with a person and not get to know them well enough to know when something is wrong. Even when they say nothing is wrong.

"Mmhm!" she hummed to let him know she knew he was lying. She had been around him counting enough money to know it sometimes came up short. Never by too much so he had a quick remedy. "Just cover it."

"Word," he may have said even though he didn't agree. Some shorts were mere miscounts or miscalculations. No big deal. Others were blatant 'fuck you' and this was seeming like the latter.

His reputation as the dragon slayer kept most people honest but sometimes, time makes some people forget. The newest addition to the Buddha crew was from his old block on Jerome avenue. They had been slinging dope when he and Manny were still stealing their daily bread but had eventually come into the fold of the Buddha crew.

Rip they took seriously but since they watched Trouble grow up, not so much. Now that Rip had moved up and wasn't coming around the money started getting funny. Trouble's first mistake was making up for the short with his own bread. Shit happens and people miscount so he always made sure the books were balanced like E-baby had taught him.

"Mmhm," she hummed knowingly with the knowingness that he could and would handle it.

The kid was becoming quite the businessman from listening to his mentors' conversations over the years. Some people talk when they should be listening but he wasn't one of them. Anytime he was around Buddha and Rip he kept his mouth shut and ears open. There would be no more formal schooling for him so he soaked up their real life experiences.

"Anyway, I need to cook," he said, which was her cue to leave. She didn't mind bringing the baby to the apartment filled with coke and cash but got ghost when he cooked crack.

"I'm going shopping with Tara and Miss Denise?" she asked as she stood since she too learned a thing or two from being around the older chicks. Chrissy and the other young girls couldn't teach her anything about anything so they had nothing to talk about anymore.

"A'ight baby," he answered and gave her an inch of bills. It was plenty so she planted a kiss on his lips and pushed the stroller from the apartment.There was plenty of coke already cooked so he focussed on the latest dilemma.

Travis had practically raised Trouble before Buddha came along so he wanted to give back once he was in the position to do so. What better way to give back than put his old block on the winning team. It came back to bite him with Manny and looked like it was about to bite him again.

"Fuck! Fuck!" he shouted once for his own complacency at giving Travis the next kilo before counting his money.

Little did he know the man planned to gun him down and take it if he did.Trouble was still too young and naive to realize you can't pull gutta niggas out the gutter no matter how hard you try. There's a reason they were in the gutter in the first place. Because they're some gutter ass, nothing ass, gutta ass niggas who are right where they're supposed to be.

The second fuck was at the personal loss he was about to take since he would make up for the short out of his own money. Everyone played their position and the money was his. It would not be short, ever. He was making plenty of money and would replenish the loss in a couple of days. It was the principle that pissed him off.

His head nodded at the thought of buying a whole nigga for a few thousand dollars. Pride scrunched his face and shook his head until reason was dislodged. He had been tried and if he didn't do anything about it he would be tried again. Trouble locked up and hit the stairwell to talk to Rip but he was heading to the elevator with Jeanine.

"Got a sec B?" he asked anyway and wasn't surprised by the answer.

"Nope! Handle it," Rip said and pressed the elevator call button. He had moved up to more money, more problems so he couldn't be bothered. "Whatever it is, you got it."

Trouble sighed at the vote of confidence but still chose option two. Buddha may have been mostly out of the game but his occasional two cents still made dollars. He was right down the hall so he rang the bell a few times.

"Sup yo?" Buddha demanded with frustration on his face and pen in hand. "It better be important cuz this class is kicking my ass!"

"Nah B. Good luck!" he said and spun on his heels. His mentors were on to bigger and better things but he still had some street shit to handle before he could get to that point. If he wanted to be a full partner one day he would have to prove his worth.

An idea popped in his head but he wasn't sure if it was a good one or not. There was only one way to find out so he headed out of the building and into the projects. He stopped by the bodega for peace offerings since it's rude to show up empty handed.

"Trouble? What's up B?" Lil Bam asked and stood when he saw the kid approaching. He flexed his body to feel the weight of the gun in his back just in case Trouble needed him to bust something. Besides him being the underboss the two teens were close. "Err thing good yo?"

"Hell yeah! Wifey out shopping so I had a break," he explained and held up the two twenty two ounce bottles of malt liquor. They went well with the blunt he pulled from behind his ear.

"Say word!" Bam cheered. He had plenty of his own weed to smoke but did enjoy the prestigious company. Trouble had become a legend in Highbridge even if his old block didn't get the memo.

"I see shit is booming yo!" Trouble acknowledged of the brisk drug activity all around them.

"Word!" he shot back proudly. He had a right to be proud since his crew was all eating and there was no violence associated with the drug trade in the projects. Part of the credit went to Bam, the rest was because of the local legend who grew up here. Which was exactly why the kid was here. They kicked it for a few blunts before it was time to get back to the White building. Which meant it was time to get to the point.

"Yo, that dude ain't around, no where?" Trouble asked and glanced around casually.

"Who?" Lil Bam wondered and looked around too.

"Bruh," he said, like the name was hard to get out. He managed to get it out but it was just a whisper. "Killa..."

"Ion know?" Bam asked and looked up at Miss Deidra's window.

"Oh, a'ight then B. I'm about to bounce," Trouble announced and stood. Bam stood with him and sent him off with a dap and hug.

Trouble didn't get what he came for but he was good and high. He wore a silly grin on his face as he descended the hill from the projects and cut through the alley where they set up shop. A whistle altered the workers to his presence and they all flocked around to make sure everything was good. There were different whistles for different things but this one alerted them to Trouble. Good trouble, so no one pulled their burners.

"What up tho!" Trouble greeted and gave pounds all around. The spot grinded to a halt as they all kicked it for a few minutes. He didn't want to interrupt the flow of business so he gave another round of pounds and headed back inside. He rode the elevator up to his floor and headed down the hall.

"It's the ten crack commandments..." he rapped as he entered the darkened apartment. He was up to number four as he closed the door and someone joined the chorus.

"I know you heard this before, never get high on your own supply..." the intruder rapped along with him. Tried to anyway because the look on the kid's face cracked him up.

"What are you doing here?" Trouble asked after nearly having a heart attack.

"Wasn't you just looking for me?" Killa reminded.

"Huh? Oh, yeah. But..." Trouble stammered and wondered if the dude didn't have some mythical, supernatural powers. He didn't since he just so happened to come out just after Trouble left. Bam told him he asked about him so he came over and used a pass key to get inside.

"So..." Killa asked with a smirk since he liked the kid. He liked Buddha and Rip as well since they were stand up guys. The world needs more stand up guys in it. Little did anyone know back then that a generation of fuck boys were up next.

Dudes who wore tight britches, blouses, twerked and sucked dick. That was mainly the rappers and they would set the trends. Have a whole generation of black folks thinking it's cool to get high til you die. A bunch of junkies singing and rapping about being junkies. If Killa had a crystal ball he might have gone to the daycare and smothered most of them now.

"Huh? Oh, yeah!" Trouble cheered when he remembered what he wanted. "So, I put some older heads from my old block on and..."

"And they shitted on you," Killa nodded knowingly. He was once a dope boy himself and knew oh so well how it worked.

"Yeah! So, what do I do?" he needed to know.

"Ion know what you do," the legend shrugged and Trouble looked crestfallen. "I can only tell you what I would do..."

Chapter 7

"Dang boy!" Keisha cheered after Trouble knocked her boots the way boots are supposed to be knocked.

"Word," he agreed with a verbal pat on his own back. And guys deserve a pat on the back when they do a bang up job in the box. Which of course is its own reward.

"Ion know what got into you!" she huffed gratefully. She only asked so he could get some more and beat it up like that every time.

"You babe," he replied and it was partially true. The other part was getting schooled by a legend. "Come on ma, I'll walk you home."

"Word cuz my moms swears she's not no baby sitter!" she laughed. It was funny since she really was a baby sitter. It's just part of being a grandma. The woman also claimed on more than one occasion that she wasn't none of Keisha's little friends but she was her best friend now.

"Word," he replied and grabbed clothes.

"Um, what you got going on?" she wondered when he dressed in all black from boots to beanie.

"Oh, nothing," he said and tucked a matching black nine millimeter in his waist.

"Just be careful Mr oh nothing!" she fussed but Keisha wasn't the fussy type when it came to him.

"Word," he replied and didn't register another word she spoke until they reached her door. He peeped in on his son and cracked a wide grin. Being someone's father made tonight's business that much more pressing so he pressed on.

'This shit works...' Trouble mused to himself as he was able to blend into the night.

He glided by quite a few people who didn't even notice him.He hit 167 street and headed over to those long ass steps. They hit differently coming up than going down so he reached the bottom effortlessly. A cab could do but he preferred to hoof it over to Jerome ave on foot. He circled the block from a block away and eased in under the shadow.

"Yo! This shit is booming B!" Travis cheered as he made another sale. Still trouble wasn't sure if he meant the brisk business or the actual product since he was taking big pulls off a woolie blunt. He could hear it sizzle loudly every time he took a pull. That would definitely explain why he was coming up short lately as well.

"And you wanted to wack the little nigga!" Maestro laughed and shook his head. He certainly wasn't with it since the kid put them on to a better product at a lower price.

"Cuz, i know that nigga the one who slumped Manny on the roof B!" he revealed and took another pull. "As long as he taking short money I'ma let him live tho."

"Ion know yo?" his partner said, twisting his lips. "Little man was living foul. He was begging to get wacked."

"Still gonna squeeze the little nigga. Fuck him, Buddha, Highbridge..." he rambled between tokes. He was still fucking the world as trouble walked up. Literally and figuratively since it was Trouble with the gun by his side. "Fuck west coast rap, fuck..."

"I fuck with Easy E tho," Trouble interjected causing him to choke on his coke smoke."Fuck you gonna do with that?" Travis laughed. "In front of all these witnesses! Nigga I'll..."

Travis was about to tell him about he would take the gun from him and shove it up his ass. Yada, yada, yada, but took a slug from the tip instead. The slug tore through his forehead and splatted the rest of his statement on the brick building behind him. His legs gave and he sat down, dead on the spot.

"What witnesses?" Trouble asked Maestro and the others present.

"Ain't nobody even out here!" he assured him as a whiff of smoke billowed from the barrel of the gun.

"I ain't seen shit! Fuck that nigga! I never liked that nigga anyway!" the others declared.

"Now, who's gonna handle the block from now on?" Trouble asked at Maestro.

"I got it," he assured and nodded vigorously.

"Good. You're short on the last pack. Make it up on the next..." the young killer said over his shoulder as he walked away. All eyes were on him until he disappeared when they blinked.

A smile spread on Trouble's face as he recalled the advice he received from the legend. Killa didn't tell him what to do, just what he would do if it were him. Namely pop the nigga's top in front of everyone and how they would never be short again.

They weren't either since Maestro not only counted it and delivered it himself, he always tossed in an extra couple hundred to keep his thoughts from being splattered on a wall too. That wasn't the only gangster shit going on in the city.

*****

"That's it, right there..." Bull said as El crept up the suburban street. He pointed at a well maintained suburban house with a Suburban parked in the driveway.

"Never would have thunk it," El nodded since this was a great place to use as a stash spot. He looked around and made sure the coast was clear before parking out front. This was a hush job so he screwed the silencer on the tip of his gun before reaching for the door.

"You won't need that. Crystal will just give it up," Bull reported and smirked at the unintended double entendre.

The middle aged white lady who maintained Queen's stash spot would gladly give herself to Bull whenever he came to pick up drugs or drop off cash. This was the last of the stash spots they had hit in the same day so Queen would be wiped out before she got the news. Bull killed two birds with one stone at each of the other spots since he stole the work and cash as well as murdered her soldiers.

"Just in case..." El said and nodded at the door handle to make him go first like they did at the last few spots. Bull sighed and got out to lead the way up to the house. He let out a soulful sigh hoping this wouldn't ruin his hit and run relationship with Crystal. It probably would since chicks don't like getting robbed at gunpoint. Girls can be funny like that.

"Who!" Crystal sang happily as she approached the front door. She peered through the window on the door and smiled at her favorite pick up man. He always dropped off some dick when he came through to drop off cash or pick up kilos of coke.

"It's me," Bull croaked since treachery didn't sit well with him. She was all smiles and throbbing vagina when she pulled the door open but both came to a sudden stop when El appeared from behind him.

"What's going on Bull?" she pleaded and raised her hands.

"I'm the one with the gun!" El reminded since she should have been asking him.

"We need to get everything. All of it..." he said with a wink. He would give up the coke and save the money for himself. He may as well have said it out loud since Bull saw the wink.

"I don't like secrets..." El advised and fired a whispered shot into Bull's winker. The hot spray of blood and brain matter splattered her face and made her swoon. El could only shake his head when the woman fainted next to the dead man. He got a chance to look up her skirt while she was laid out and nodded. "Bitch fine tho..."

"Huh? I..." Crystal moaned when she awoke a few minutes later. El knew from the last few spots that the deep freezers contained the coke so he stacked the kilos next to the door.

"I'ma need that money Miss. The one he winked about," he said and nodded towards the dead guy.

"I don't..." she began but the gun began to rise towards her face. "Oh, the money! Follow me..."

"Don't mind if I do..." El said and cracked half a smile as her ass shifted under the skirt. Crystal caught a glimpse of him looking at her ass as she led him into the bedroom.

"Under there," Crystal said, pointing at the bed.

"Yeah right!" he laughed at the notion of him ducking under the bed so she could get the drop on him. "You get it!"

"Ok!" she moaned and got on her hands and knees. She put that back shot arch in her back as she reached under the bed. Her skirt rose up enough for him to get a good look at the fat crotch under the yellow panties.

"Ok then!" he cheered of the first stack of cash she tossed out behind her. It and her fat box was enough of a distraction for her to make her move. Crystal tossed the next stack of cash a little further, knowing his eyes would follow. She dropped flat on her stomach and rolled over on her back while raising the gun.

El got off a silent shot but the gun was pointed where she was a second ago instead of where she was now. Her gun was pointed right at his chest and knocked a hole in his heart. The clock was now ticking so she collected the million from under the bed and her few favorite outfits. They took a few trips to the Suburban before she could pull away from the suburbs and start a new life somewhere else with a million dollar headstart.

Chapter 8

"Babe?" Jeanine asked like she does when she wants to talk business. She used a different tone when she wanted some dick. He had just flown down to spend some time with her since her due date was near.

"Sup yo?" he asked since he was looking for an opportunity to broach the subject of business anyway.

"My people say the dope ain't doping like it's supposed to?" she asked even though it wasn't a question. Her girls had already asked the questions, she needed answers.

"The fuck that supposed to mean?" he laughed.

"The shit ain't cooking up right," she said straight to the point.

"Cuz that shit be cut! Niggas be cutting that shit to the bone! Time it hit the pot half the coke replaced with cut," Rip reminded.

"Yeah, except this your shit. Straight from your people," Jeanine replied. She was halfway out of the game herself but still directed traffic from the sideline.

"Word! I'll holla at cuz," he sighed since he hated having to talk to Carlos. Dude was getting weirder by the day. Still, he was insulation for the crew since Joey ran all sales through him.

It was the right plan but the wrong man because Carlos was now scooping twenty percent off the top and replacing it with cut. That's on top of the ten percent Joey was taking, plus an additional ten percent Jeannie's ex-girlfriend was taking before she distributed it to the other girls. It was a wonder how the dope was doping at all with all those steps.

"Yeah cuz, Mika said half the shit just disappeared when it hit the water!" she relayed and watched his face go sour at the mention of the name. She was Jeanine's ex and he always scowled at her name.

"Ion, even know why you're still doing the shit? Not for money! I keep you laced," he got around to where he wanted to go. "It's time to let that shit go ma!"

"You do keep me laced. For a boyfriend. But until I have a ring on my finger, I gotta do for self," she sighed. "Plus, them chicks would be lost without me!"

"Fuck them chicks! Them bitches will be just fine without you!" he declared and he was correct because needy people will always find someone to need. People always swear they can't do without a person until they have to do without that person. Come to find out most times they make out just fine.

"Mmhm," she hummed and smiled at his skipping over the point about the ring. She knew he loved her as much as he knew how and would accept that from him. On cue a strong contraction doubled her over.

"What?" he asked wide eyed. For all of his kids this was the first time he had actually been around when the woman went into labor. Until now that is.

"Ugh!" she moaned and had a better idea than moaning. "Mama!"

"Yes!" her mother called back as she rushed to investigate. She too knew her daughter's different tone and this one was a new one. She knew exactly what it was when she saw the fluid running down her legs. "Girl, your water done broke!"

"Let's ride" Rip proclaimed and scooped Jeanine off of her feet. He was happy to be in a rental so she wouldn't be leaking on his leather seats. Her mother climbed into the back seat and they were off.

"You finna make the baby fall out the way you mashing the gas, then brakes!" Mama fussed as Rip dipped the whip through town.

"This is how we drive to the A&P in New York!" he laughed while Jeanine practiced her breathing techniques.He came to a screeching halt in front of the hospital and hopped out to come around and let the women out. They were met by a wheelchair and she was rushed up to the maternity ward. Rip decided to skip the actual birth and paced the waiting room like they did on the TV shows he grew up on.

His mind was all over the place but occasionally stopped like a roulette wheel on different people, places and things. Jeanine had been stressing him about getting married but he had resisted. Now he wasn't sure why since he loved her and she was giving life in his name. Monte and his mother were married. Buddha and Tara, even Trouble vowed to marry Keisha when they turned eighteen.

"I'ma do that shit!" he determined. His lips twisted at the timing, plus no way was he going to top Buddha's surprise wedding in the park. He resumed his pacing until a foreign language caught his attention. A smile twisted the corner of his mouth as he sprang into action.

"What the..." a man grunted when Rip snatched him by the arm. The man protested and squirmed as he drug him up to the maternity ward.

"What the..." the doctor wanted to know too when they burst into the delivery room. All eyes were on them including Jeanine with her feet in stirrups.

"Rip!" she reeled at the stranger with a good view of her open legs. The man accidentally looked and turned beet red from embarrassment.

"Found a preacher!" Rip cheered and held the man's hand up like he just won a prize fight.

"Uh, Rabbi!" the man corrected and flipped his curly sideburns.

"You can still marry us can't you!" Rip demanded. He didn't know much about religion but enough to know there is only one God.

"Technically, I guess, I mean..." the Rabbi stammered with his head nodding. That was enough for Jeanine's mother.

"Let's get it!" she cheered and took the position by her daughter.

"I'm working here?" the doctor reminded as the nurses gushed romantically.

"Yeah, you giving the bride away!" Jeanine's mother barked."I'll have to do it from here since she's crowning," the man agreed. He would definitely do his part to bring a child into the world in wedlock.

They just managed to get to their 'I do's' when Gabriel junior entered the world. On cue Rip's pager went off. Everyone on the planet would have to wait but seeing

Buddha's code to an unknown number. He wanted to share the good news so he made the call.

"Yo! Bust it!" They both shouted into the phone at the same time. Neither yielded so they continued to speak at the same time. "I got a son B! Word! That's dope!"

"Oh and..." Rip added since he was able to one up his best friend. "We just got married yo!"

"Word! That's dope!" Buddha congratulated and smiled down at his family. Life was good, but would it last?

*****

"What up tho?" Rip asked when Joey's door was pulled open. He did a double take at the white girl wearing nothing but a wife beater. Big nipples pressed through the thin fabric and made him look at the number on the door to remember where he was.

"He's in the bathroom," she said and turned. Rip watched her ass jiggle under the thin shirt until he shook it off. His thumb rubbed the wedding band on his index finger and remembered his wife.

"You ever had some Italy pussy my nigga!" Joey laughed as he came out of the back.

"Italian and yeah," Rip replied and looked at the girl. She didn't take the message so he expounded, "Beat it!"

"What's up yo?" Joey asked after watching the ass jiggle out of the room. He had free reign down here so he wondered which one of his misdeeds this was about. So he tried to change the subject. "Congrats on the kid yo! And you got married too!"

"Word!" Rip replied and had to stop and smile at the family at the house. He drifted into his head for a second and smiled. Until he realized he got got. "Yo, people complaining about the work? Said it's not coming back like it should?"

"Who? When! What!" Joey reeled incredulously. Ten percent was nothing and he knew it since most coke was much less pure than that.

"My girl, wife's people is who," he explained. A smirk lifted the corner of his lip briefly at having a wife. No more wifey, she was his wife."

"I don't know how? Shit pure when I bring it down?" Joey wondered.

"Carlos," they both guessed but only one was half right. Carlos was the distributor once Joey brought the work down south. He was tapping the package after Joey took out his ten percent. Each hand it touched stepped on it until it was forty percent pure by the time it reached noses and veins.

"I'm just gonna cut son off yo," Joey decided and shrugged. It was an easy decision since Carlos's racket was fucking with his.

"Nah, that's bruh fam. Just gotta tell his ass to stop," Rip sighed since he would have to be the one to talk to him. He really tried to avoid talking to him as much as possible even if his Newport News buyer was buying more and more weight. "We both gonna push up on him and tell him to knock it off! He eating good as fuck already!"

"Word," Joey agreed. He would talk to Carlos as well since it was threatening to expose his own skimming operations. He had a nice little side hustle with the white girl who had her ear pressed against the bedroom door right now. She allowed him access to the suburbs who were still paying a hundred and twenty five dollars a gram. The least he could do was keep theirs pure since he was making over a hundred grand off each kilo he pulled off the top.

"Anyway, I bet you ain't hittin that right!" Rip laughed as he stood to leave. "White girls like it rough!"

"All girls like it rough," Joey called after him as he departed. He may or may not have been correct but one thing for sure was he loved it down here.

Rip did too but his duties kept him on the move. After leaving Joey he headed back over to the apartment complex where they first started trapping. They had left the daily sales alone once they started selling weight to Ace but Ace was gone and Carlos ran the trap.

"What the actual fuck!" Rip reeled when he saw the chaos at the complex. It always had a steady flow but now it was wide open like a bazaar.

People walked around selling weed, coke, crack and pussy like it was now legal. A police car pulled in and Rip started to pull away until Black-magic jumped into the passenger seat. Her head disappeared from sight when she went down on the cop.

"This shit is wide the fuck open!" Rip fumed and stomped towards Ace's old apartment. He could hear the music booming from the walk and saw weed smoke seeping from cracks in the wall. He would kick the door down if it hadn't been unlocked, but it was, so he walked right in.

"What up tho!" Carlos cheered as he multitasked. He had one stripper dancing on the coffee table with another blowing him on the sofa. He drank a beer with one hand while the other held a thick blunt.

"Get the fuck out!" Rip shouted but the strippers turned their noses up at him. One popped the dick out of her mouth to pose a question.

"Who this nigga think he is coming up in your trap telling people what to do?" the one on her knees wanted to know.

"Bitch..." Rip growled and snatched the gun from his waist. Good thing she used to be a track star and was able to get up and out before getting herself shot.

"See how that hoe hurdled that coffee table B!" Carlos laughed and took a pull and another sip.

"Ok, first of all, put your dick up!" Rip shouted and went over to turn the music off so he wouldn't have to keep shouting.

"My bad..." he laughed and tucked himself away. "Sup yo?"

"Tell me you ain't got the work in here, and you wide the fuck open like this!" Rip demanded and looked around. There were empty bottles, blunt roaches and food boxes everywhere but he didn't see any dope.

"Hell naw! I keep that shit at my mama house!" he proudly proclaimed as if storing kilos of coke in your mama's house was a good thing. Rip could only shake his head and move on to the next issue.

"And stop stepping on shit nigga!" Rip stated plainly. Had he asked, he would have lied so he skipped over all of that. "If you want to pay up front then you can do whatever the fuck you want to do! As long as you represent the Buddha crew, that shit stays raw!"

"Bet," Carlos agreed and lowered his head. The act of contrition was a good look but he wasn't going to stop. Not with the latest bullshit he added to his batch of bullshit. "G-money wanna meet up again?"

"With me? For what?" Rip reeled. He was steadily moving up and had no need to consort with mid level dealers.

"He says he tryna spend some real bread. I told him he gotta talk to you directly. I can't negotiate on your behalf now can I?" Carlos dared since he knew the answer.

"No you can't. And bruh can keep dealing with you, or find another route," Rip shot back. Greed got the best of him a second later so he compromised. "Take him to meet Joey."

"Bet!" Carlos quickly agreed since G-money had been insisting on moving up the ladder. He kept asking about Buddha but this was a step closer to the top. He reached out to dap Rip up but got left hanging.

"Yeah, bet," he replied and headed back out to his car.

"Sucka ass nigga," Carlos snarled at Rip as his car pulled away from the complex. As soon as it was clear he lifted the sofa cushion to reveal stacks of cocaine. He pulled out a package of cooked coke and dumped some on the table. Once he loaded a chunk onto his pipe he pulled a lighter and took a long sizzling pull to add to his troubles.

Sa'id Salaam

Chapter 9

"Hello Casper," Pope sighed. He hated calling the man for anything, especially for more help.

The battle for Brooklyn and Queens between him and Queen was getting him nowhere. He was spending more on funerals than he was making from drugs. The final straw was when Queen had his mother shot down coming out of church. As bad as he wanted to fuck her, now it was just fuck her.

"How can I help you Mr Pope?" the white leader of the Black Mob sang sarcastically.

He was watching the back and forth battle like a match at the US Open. It didn't matter who won the various battles since he planned to win the war. His competitors were weakening themselves and would not be able to put up any resistance when he scooped in to claim the throne for himself.

"Can you send that hitter again? This bitch done killed my moms!" Pope moaned like a wounded animal. Which he was and nothing is more dangerous than a wounded animal.

"Uh, no she's booked pretty solid at the moment," he lied since Yolo was busy prancing around the house like a lunatic. "Don't forget, you did kill her child..."

"Shit! I can't keep losing my men!" he protested.

"You should take matters into your own hands. You can't kill one woman?" Casper chided to get a rise out of the man.

"Of course I can! I..." he proclaimed until he realized he was the only one on the line. As soon as he sat the receiver back in its cradle it began to ring again. "Hello?"

"We need to talk!" Queen barked.

"You killed my mother and now you want to talk!" Pope shot back hotly.

"Yeah, you killed my son too. We're both losing men, blocks, customers," she reminded. At the end of the day they were drug dealers and neither was selling many drugs. Now Giggles had slid his own crew out there to take up the slack.

"How do I know you won't try nothing?" he wanted to know.

"Because I'll be at the Waldorf. Alone. No men, no weapons," she explained. "And I'm horny!"

"What!" he reeled in disbelief. As long as he had been trying to fuck her and now she wants to give it up after killing his mother.

"Check your email..." she advised and waited. Queen smirked when she heard him gasps at the picture she had just sent of her freshly shaven vagina.

"I'll be there!" he insisted and hung up. A smile spread on his face at finally being able to kill two birds with one stone. If she was horny he was going to fuck her real good, then kill her. He picked the phone back up and put his plan in motion.

A few hours later he arrived at the iconic hotel for a second time for the day. This time Queen was waiting in the lobby as agreed. She was alone and unarmed besides the skin tight tube dress showing off her dangerous curves.

"Fuck!" Pope exclaimed as he ran his eyes over her voluptuous body.

"Unarmed..." she said and gave a slow motion twirl to prove it. The dress couldn't conceal a dime let alone a weapon of any kind. Pope couldn't decide what to focus on from the fat ass or the mounds of good titty meat squeezed from the top of the dress.

"Likewise..." he offered and lifted his hands. Her eyes zoomed in on the lump in his slacks and tilted her head. She reached out to investigate for herself and grabbed it.

"Oh my," Queen reeled when she realized it was a really hard dick. It throbbed in her hand as she held it. "You sure this won't hurt me?"

"Nah, I know what to do with it. Now can I peek in your purse?" he asked even though the tiny designer bag couldn't hold a gun. A straight razor perhaps but there was nothing inside but her insulin.

"You can hold it if..." she offered but he declined.

"Let's get a room..." Pope offered. He walked over to the counter and went through the motions to get the same room he already rented for the night. He paid the thousand dollar fee once again but this one went into the clerks pocket. "Send us up a bottle of champagne. And a couple of steaks."

"Nice touch," Queen agreed as he extended his elbow like a gentleman. She accepted it and was escorted to the elevator. "A truce is in our best interest?"

"Going back to making money sure sounds good to me," he agreed as they ascended. "Now we just need to pound out the details..."

"A good pounding sure sounds good to me!" Queen purred and turned to face him. Pope leaned in and grabbed two handfuls of ass and slid his tongue into her ready mouth. They moaned, groaned and grinded until they reached their floor. They rolled along the wall, engaged in a lip lock until they reached the door. Pope fumbled with the key and finally got the door open. He couldn't wait to get his dick inside of her but first had to get inside of the room.

"Don't worry, I know how to get it in," he assured her.

"No worries, it gets so blood clot wet you won't 'ave no problems," she assured him. They bypassed the sofa and headed straight for the bedroom.

"My goodness!" Pope exclaimed when she peeled off the dress and showed the most beautiful body he had ever seen. Her fat vagina almost looked like fist holding the black power sign.

"Not too shabby yourself!" Queen cheered when he came out of his clothes. Pope sported the average dad bod but a very impressive erection that leaned left like a road sign pointing to a curve ahead.

Queen decided to take him up on his threats to suck her pussy inside out. She climbed on the middle of the bed and spread her legs and labia. There was a tense moment as he approached and she dug into her purse. Not that the insulin could hurt him since she injected a dose into her stomach. Next out the tiny bag were two tubes of flavored gel.

"Cherry or berry?" Queen offered and held out the tubes of pussy flavoring.

"Berry!" he cheered and cheesed and she squirted the content on her vagina. He leaned in and gave a lick that arched her back clean off the mattress.

"Bumba clot!" Queen cursed him and her dead husband for never eating the pussy.

"Bumba clit!" Pope shot back when her clitoris popped out like a Jack in the box. He knew what to do with and ran his tongue around, over and under it like a Kansas twister.

"Mi can't..." Queen was trying to say but forgot what it was. Instead she just grunted and bust a good blot clot nut in his mouth.

"Mmhm, tried to tell you!" he chuckled proudly at his handiwork. He was about to talk his shit but she pulled his face back into her soaked snatch for more. A few more revolutions of his tongue and she bust off again.

"Blood fiyah! Buck! Buck Buck!" Queen cheered and licked shots with her finger pointed like a gun.

"Now for the..." Pope was saying until a deep yawn interrupted him. He tried to shake it off and continue, "The, the dick!"

"That's a nice, big one!" she cheered as he wagged his curved dick. "Too bad you don't 'ave enough time to get im wet."

"I..." Pope was saying but got paused by yet another deep yawn. He felt suddenly more tired than he ever felt in his life. A sense of panic swept in when he figured out why. What he wanted to know was, "How?"

"Should 'ave pick cherry ya know!" Queen laughed. The cherry flavored gel contained the same poison but she just wanted to send him off with a guilt trip. Her so-called insulin shot was an antidote to prevent it from working on her. "Berry dem poison!"

"I, I, I..." he tried to say but was going to have to take it with him wherever he was going. "Mi can't 'ear you, ya know!" Queen teased but dead people don't mind being teased since they can't hear it. A chime of the door alerted her but she wasn't concerned since not even her own people knew where she was. After Bull's betrayal she moved in silence amongst her own people.

She wrapped that fine frame in one of those thick ass Waldorf Astoria robes and jiggled over to the door. Her legs wobbled when she stood from that good nut that made her look down at the dick. She could only shake her head and answer, "Oo knock 'pon da door?"

"Room service!" came the reply that got the door pulled open. A smile spread on her face as the stainless steel domes were pushed inside. A bottle of Dom was chilling in a bucket of ice.

"Ere you go..." Queen tried to tip but the man politely declined.

"No thanks, I've already been taken care of..." he said as he rushed from the room. Queen thought the big titties peeking from the robe had run him off. It wouldn't be the first time.

"Bumba clot!" she laughed at her own sexual prowess as well as the free steak dinner. The stainless steel room service dome gave a little resistance when she tried to lift it off. Nothing a good tug couldn't fix so she tugged it. Then realized the resistance came courtesy of the wire connected to the pin on the grenade.

"Bumba clot!" she repeated but this one would be her last. The device detonated a second later since Pope wasn't alive to make sure it didn't. He got his money's worth even in death when the shrapnel shredded Queen to pretty pieces.

*****

"Flaco, Brian, Roberto..." Giggles called out as he looked around the packed apartment. The named men had to keep their emotions in check since they had been called to do something they didn't want to do.

"Si, ok, bet," they all agreed when he finished naming the names of the men he was sending out to Queens and Brooklyn.

There was a power struggle going on so he would send some of his own men out to both boroughs and control the street sales. It was good for close to a million a day but Miguel would have never made the move himself.

Nor would Buddha since they were both too smart to do something that stupid. Local dealers were busy shooting at each other so he would set up shop right on the border. The violence should drive all traffic straight to them. In theory it should work but reality is a different story.

"W,w,w,we, n, ne, need some g, guns!" Roberto moaned and the other men around the room shook their heads.

"You do? Here, take mine..." Giggles said with a smirk as he pulled the Desert Eagle Buddha once gifted to Miguel.

"Um?" Roberto asked unsurely after seeing the looks on faces after the cowardly outburst.

Being scared is natural but showing it was forbidden. He still reached for the offer before Giggles tilted the huge barrel up towards his face. The fifty caliber sounded like a bomb going off in the small apartment. Shirts, jeans and sneakers were ruined when he popped his top, causing his brains to shower the room like confetti.

"So, Queens right boss?" Flaco nodded agreeably.

"Yeah! You need a g,g,g, gun too?" Giggles dared and turned the hand cannon in that direction causing everyone to duck.

"No!" the rest of the armed men shouted and hit the door. In truth they were better off trying their luck with Giggles and the canon since someone knew they were on the way.

The men loaded up a whole kilo of cooked coke, guns and snorted a few lines of powdered courage up their nostrils and headed out. They had rented rooms in a hotel that hugged the border of both boroughs. It should be far enough away from the fighting so they could focus on sales. In theory anyway.

"Ok, you guys spread out," Flaco directed since someone had to. He posted gunners on all four corners, and runners to hit the block and steer traffic. Once word spread of the huge vials coming from the hotel the spot would be booming.

"Genius!" Brian cheered once they were alone in the room with a mountain of crack. This would be headquarters where they could collect the money and supply the troops.

"Because I am a genius!" Flaco shot back smugly. He was pretty proud of himself and he had good reason since the plan was working.

Nearly an hour later and the dealers were dropping off cash and picking up more G-packs. The theory was working well until it came to a screeching halt. The drop offs and re-up came to an abrupt end and the noise of drug dealing was muted.

"The fuck?" Brian was the first to notice since Flaco was romancing a new boricua mami on the phone.

"Un momento..." Flaco told the girl when he picked up on the sudden silence as well. He made a motion towards the gun on the table and directed, "See what's going on?"

"Me?" Brian asked but there was no one else in the room. He heard the cowardly tone in his voice and thought about Roberto's brains dripping from the ceiling. That's why he inhaled and exhaled a sigh before picking up the gun and heading to the door.

"Huh?" he asked when he stepped outside and saw nothing and no one.

The last time he looked out there were lines of junkies for each dealer. Now he looked left, right and left again but didn't see a soul. Brian was about to head back inside to make his report until he saw a pretty girl pop out of one of the rooms. Whatever was going would probably still be going on after he got a little brown sugar. And this caramel colored chick sure looked sweet.

"Hey handsome..." she beckoned with a smile and he came over."You ain't seen my friends out here have you?" he asked as he approached. "Some boricuas?"

"Yup. They're in here..." she sang and flashed a smile that sucked him in even more.

"They are?" Brian asked incredibly since they were twenty deep out here.

"Yup," she nodded and stepped aside so he could enter the darkened room. The coppery smell of fresh blood stopped him in his tracks but it was too late.

"Ok, bye-bye," the pretty girl sang as the room flashed with the silent shot from her gun. The bodies of all the dead Camacho soldiers littered the room but Brian didn't get to see them since he joined them. The girl did a little happy dance and left the room. She skipped down the walkway and knocked on the door where Flaco was still verbally seducing the new chick in his life.

"Fuck!" he fussed at the interruption and got up from the bed. He stomped over and snatched the door open to fuss at Brian for not using the key. Instead he found the same pretty girl smiling up at him. "Let me call you back..."

"Can I come in?" she asked and he snatched her inside before pushing the door closed.

"You tryna make a few dollars?" Flaco asked since a bird in the hand beat the one on the phone back in Harlem.

"Nah, Casper already paid me," she shrugged. The name twisted his face and made him look at the gun he left on the nightstand. The girl watched his eyes and pulled her own gun from behind her back. The long silencer tip touched his nose when he turned back.

"You got it mami!" he quickly conceded since she clearly had the drop on him. He nodded towards the bag of cash on the table. Then guesstimated if he could reach his gun when she went for the money. It was fifty/fifty which was a lot better odds than dealing with Giggles if he came back empty handed.

"I believe you have drugs too?" she asked and inhaled deeply like she could smell it. That much coke sure does have a smell so she smiled and nodded. "Yup, you got drugs!"

"Giggles is going to kill me!" he pleaded.

"What do you think I'm going to do if you don't?" she asked and tilted her head curiously. She could tell he was still on the fence so she sweetened the deal. "Tell you what, hand over the drugs and I'll let you go with your friends?"

"Bet!" he agreed since he would just blame everything on Brian. He carefully picked up the tote bag containing the change from the kilo and tossed it at her feet. Then let out a sigh as the gun at his face began to lower.

"Tell your friends Yolo said hello..." the lovely little lunatic sang and fired a shot at the floor.

Flaco looked down as the gun came back up. He just saw the barrel before it sparked and made everything go dark. Yolo loaded up the drugs and money and left a mess behind. The Black Mob had officially claimed Brooklyn and Queens as their own and Giggles was going to hear about it.

Sa'id Salaam

Chapter 10

New York didn't feel the same when Rip's flight began to descend to LaGuardia airport. It was exactly the same, the only difference was he had left his heart in Richmond. He let out a deep sigh since it was what it was. Jeanine found the perfect house to house the family so he had to work to pay for it.

At least that was his excuse since he had plenty of money put up. He and Buddha had bought their second building in the hood. That just gave him another excuse to keep grinding until he had enough money for a third. The thing about greed is they still haven't printed enough money to satisfy it.

"You know a good spot to eat in the city?" the pretty stewardess asked as they began to deplane. She had been eyeing him or his chain since they boarded in Richmond so he wondered when she would get around to pushing up.

"No!" he shouted and shot her down like the Atari asteroids game they grew up on. She looked confused by the outburst so he lifted his diamond studded wedding band to explain, "Fuck outa here!"

"Prolly fake anyway..." she muttered as she slinked away. He should have told her to go fuck herself since that's exactly what she was going to do since she had to buy her own dinner.

Rip had to laugh at himself since he was really just mad at himself. He had to go out to Cali now and didn't know how he would hold up against that good California head. His thumb made its way back to the wedding band and soothed him. The best thing a man can have is a good wife, next to that is a solid friend. He had both in Jeanine and Buddha. Buddha was a good example in his life.

He worked hard in school as well as their business. Most of all he didn't cheat on his wife. He didn't even cheat on a real girlfriend when he had one. And the thing about a good example is that it shows you that you can too. Whatever it is, you can too.

"Word!" Rip assured himself and stuck his chest out. He marched off the plane and out of the terminal. Instead of hailing a taxi to the Bronx he caught a shuttle to the private hangars and met Giggles at the private jet.

"There he is!" a clearly drunk Giggles cheered and threw his arms wide. Two young Spanish girls giggled and cooed when they saw Rip.

"Sup B?" Rip asked in the embrace. He looked over at the young girls and knew they could only serve one purpose. His purpose was to handle the re-up so he wondered why he was here this time. "What you got going on?"

"Tranquilo papi," he replied but Rip was already calm. He just wanted to know what was going on. "I'm on a little vacation!"

"And them?" he asked since this was bad business. Young girls and millions in cash didn't mix.

"Some rec for the ride!" Giggles cheered and wobbled. They boarded the jet with the money and took their seats.

"Sit your asses down!" Rip barked when the girls wanted to dance as the plane taxied to the runway.

"He needs some pussy! Marie..." Giggles ordered and the one who went by that name approached.

"I need some sleep!" Rip corrected and shooed her away. He was the only one on the jet who actually got some sleep since he spent the week with his wife and son. By the time the flight reached cruising altitude everyone was asleep except Rip. He was alone with his thoughts and they all went back to Virginia.

Rip got into a limo when they reached LA. He and the money headed to see Don Chavez while Giggles and the girls went to a Hollywood hotel to party. He would be there all week and return when Rip came back in a week. The Camacho crew had to run itself because Giggles was too busy partying.

The limo arrived at the gated estate and once again a party was in full swing. Rip concluded that the party never stopped but also the plug never took part. His men scooped up the duffle bags of cash and led him inside to the boss.

"My friend R.I.P!" Don Chavez greeted happily. Rip noticed he always seemed so happy to see him. He was of course since he brought millions of dollars with him every time he came.

"Sup B!" Rip replied and embraced the man. They made small talk until Don Chavez swung a left turn and got serious.

"I am hearing things?" he offered and tilted his head. Rip had to let a flurry of sarcastic remarks pass before opening his mouth. Plus, everything with him was a test. He'd seen a man murdered in this same room for failing one of those tests.

Don Chavez asked his Denver dealer about the operations and got lied to. He didn't like lies so he had him un-alived right there on the spot. Rip got the message but Giggles kept on lying.

"About what?" was the safest reply Rip could think of.

He had been hearing things too and most of it wasn't good. Giggles inadvertently removed both Queen and Pope from the equation and it equalled chaos. The streets of Brooklyn and Queens were on fire as different cliques battled for the lucrative blocks. This gave the Black Mob room to slide in and take over.

"Giggles. They say he is getting reckless? Say he intervened in a local beef?" Don asked even though he had the answers already.

"I'm out of the city most of the week. I handle the Bronx and operations in Virginia," Rip replied quick enough to be believable.

Don Chavez nodded his head and accepted his answer. Which meant he passed the test and got to live. Giggles had increased revenue but was making a lot of noise doing it. The explosion that killed two known drug lords in a downtown Manhattan hotel was national news. Not to mention the plug was semi religious and didn't like how the married Giggles went wild every time he came out.

The talk shrank once again and they chopped it up while the money was counted in another room. Once it added up to what it was supposed to, the coke would be loaded in the limo for the ride back to the airport. Six hours later Rip was back in the city with hundreds of pounds of cocaine.

*****

"Yo!" Rip exclaimed as he barged into Buddha's bedroom like he had done his whole life. Except now he had a wife and child sharing it with him. They owned a couple of buildings and wanted to move but Tara wouldn't hear of it. She would not leave Denise on her own. Not to mention the built-in babysitter for the full time students.

"I know, Cali pussy squirts like pineapples when you bite into them!" Buddha mocked and laughed. The confused look on his friend's face made him laugh even harder.

"Son, who the fuck bites a pussy? That shit don't make no sense B!" Rip replied and shook his head. Once Buddha cut off the guffaws he was able to continue. "That nigga Giggles is bugging..."

Buddha just listened and learned all about the growing tension between Giggles and the connect. His tongue automatically traced the years old chips left behind from when Giggles shoved a gun into his mouth. Then took his girlfriend. He was actually delighted to hear he was spinning out of control.

"Let it play out however it plays out," Buddha advised. He had been dropping hints for his partner to leave the game but Rip wasn't hearing them. Buddha loved the influx of cash coming his way too so he didn't push the issue. If he lived long enough to have regrets this would be one of them.

"Shit B, if Giggles go down..." Rip sighed with stars in his eyes. He could clearly see the throne, with him sitting on it.

"If Giggles go down we go down," Buddha finished his statement and knocked the stars from his eyes. Rip looked confused so he gave a brief history lesson. "Frank Lucas, Nicky Barnes, Alpo. All kings of New York. All snitched on everyone when they got knocked!"

"Word?" Rip reeled since he only heard half of their stories. The good half of money, hoes and clothes. Not how niggas fold when the cell doors close.

"Word! We winning just like we are son," he reminded and turned back to his book. "This shit has to have an end."

"Word," Rip nodded and headed out of the apartment. He too knew it had to end one day but it wouldn't be today. No one was home across the hall so he hit the staircase and hopped down the few flights to see Trouble.

He eased the key in and rushed inside since he always got a kick out of seeing the startled looks on him and Keisha's faces when he barged in on them fucking. Instead the strong aroma of cocaine cooking nearly took his breath away.

"Yoooo!" Rip reeled and covered his face. Trouble rushed around the kitchen wall with an Uzi in his hand but relaxed when he saw the boss.

"Sup yo?" he questioned, muffled behind the respirator he wore while cooking up.

"Give me one..." Rip demanded and held his breath. Trouble tossed him one so he could come in and help out.

Rip generally felt helpless when he was away from Jeanine and the baby. They were home in Virginia so he made himself useful by helping the kid coke . He was impressed by the new whip technique he employed that increased the yield of the final product. Trouble could have easily cuffed the extra profits he generated but Rip and Buddha raised him right. Once they finished cooking he opened the terrace door while Trouble turned on a few fans. The crack dried while they aired the noxious fumes from the apartment.

"Deja vu.." Rip laughed as he and Trouble sat at the dining room table and stuffed crack into the vials. It was only a few years but felt like much longer.

"Word!" Trouble cheered. He listened with a wide smile as Rip reminisced on the good old days. By the time Joey rang the bell they were already up to the chance meeting in the park that changed their lives.

"Dang!" Trouble reeled at the description of how fine Jennifer used to be. She was just over three hundred pounds now as a result of three kids, spousal abuse, lack of self esteem, neglect and good cooking.

"Sup yo," Joey greeted when he opened the door for him. He dapped Trouble up as Rip nodded in reply.

"Sup B. You spit at the nigga Carlos was talmbout?" Rip greeted and asked.

"Hell yeah! Son spending big! I'm taxing his ass!" he cheered and almost said too much since he was planning on cutting G-money's coke down to seventy five percent. Which gave him one free kilo out of each four he sold.

"Word," Rip agreed and swallowed the bad feeling he felt. The money was good so he would keep it to himself. He too might regret it if he lived long enough. There are only two ways out of this game and one was worse than the other.

Dead would suck but prison is even worse.

Sa'id Salaam

Chapter 11

The next few years sped by at the speed of life and things had remained the same for the Buddha crew even if everything had changed. Buddha was almost ready to graduate while Tara was already in medical school. They both excelled in school despite giving birth to a baby girl named after her grandmother.

The family compromised on leaving Denise behind when the apartment next door became vacant and Buddha used some cash to skip the long waiting list for the unit. They moved next door so they would all still be close.Rip was still back and forth between the city and the country and managed to squeeze out another son with his wife. He also managed to keep his dick in his pants on his weekly trips to California. They were moving so much money and drugs they now had to use two jets.

Tara and Jeanine had become the best of friends since they had more than their Virginia roots in common. They were both married to best friends and business partners so it just made good sense to do the same. They opened a series of beauty salons and daycares all over Richmond. The two businesses complimented each since chicks got all glammed up to go to the club, then got pregnant. Their children were more than best friends, they were cousins.

Giggles was still partying hard and hanging onto control by a thread. Any time someone questioned his authority he murdered them. It wasn't long until people stopped questioning him. Plus they were all making money and that was all that mattered.

Don Chavez was hot about Giggles losing Brooklyn and Queens but emerging markets in DC, Baltimore and Charlotte more than made up for it. Rip assigned members of the Camacho clan to the different cities to handle the distribution. Joey was still skimming and scamming his way down south. His main customer was waiting happily when he arrived for their next transaction.

"Sup yo?" Joey asked as he walked into the hotel room for the next sale. Two years had passed since he started selling to the man but today something seemed different. Nothing he said, or could see, just something in the air. "Something wrong?"

"Wrong? Absolutely not!" G-money replied happily. He was all smiles as he handed over the money for the deal.

"A'ight yo," he shrugged and passed off the twenty kilos of coke. Actually it was only twelve pounds of actual coke and the rest was cut. As a result Joey had a nice cache of cash stocked away in the house he had built from the ground up.

"Looks like we reached our quota!" G-money cheered when he took possession of the drugs. He cast a glance at the clock but didn't notice what time it was.

"Quota?" Joey asked as he tucked the cash into a tote bag.

"Yeah. We've officially purchased enough cocaine from you to get you a life sentence," he announced and watched the man's face as he processed what he meant.

"Bruh..." Joey moaned when he got it. He looked at the clock too since he saw G-money look a few times. Now he noticed the hole above the twelve and knew it was a camera lens. His head turned towards the door with thoughts of trying his luck but his luck wore off as the door came off the hinges.

"Federal agents!" All of the many agents shouted as they stormed into the room. Joey was shoved to the ground with a knee in his neck until his hands were firmly secured behind his back. G-money gave high fives all around at the mission accomplished.

"Take him to the office. Let's go round up the rest of these guys," G-money directed as he stepped from the room. Agents were currently hitting several spots and targets at the same time but he wanted to personally hit the next spot. "Let the raids begin!"

*****

"See, now every time your ass end up pregnant again you gonna blame me!" Rip warned as Jeanine pranced around in a pair of Daisy Duke's with ass cheeks jiggling from the bottom.

"Who? What I do?" she purred and giggled since the kids were at her mother's. "I'm already pregnant again so..."

"So, this one is just practice," Rip laughed and began to pull at his zipper. It was only a few inches of zipper but he wouldn't make it.

Both Rip and Jeanine both snapped their heads towards the door when it exploded under the battering ram. Both went for their guns to fight the intrusion. They purchased the house way out in the country to prevent this but the guns were just in case they couldn't. Both had their guns up as the house filled with masked men.

"Federal agents!" they began to scream but it was too late since Jeanine had already closed her eyes and began to fire. The agents fired back and sent her back peddling into the wall.

"Drop it Rip!" G-money screamed as Rip looked at his wife sliding down the wall with holes in her torso. It was only the familiar voice that gave him pause as the red beams danced on his face and chest. He complied by tossing the gun aside and rushing to his wife.

"Breathe baby! Breathe!" he pleaded as she took labored breaths. He was quickly tackled and cuffed before Jeanine was flipped onto her stomach and cuffed as well. "The fuck yo! Call an ambulance!"

"A bus is on the way," G-money announced as he lifted his mask.

"I fucking knew it. Puto madre," Rip said, shaking his head. He had a sinking feeling from the moment he met the man but greed got the best of him like it gets the best of most. Another suspicion chased the first away and he had to ask, "Cuz put you on us? Carlos?"

"No," G-money said while his head nodded incongruently. He had zero respect for Carlos as well as a nagging suspicion that he killed his sister. He was just lucky enough not to leave a trace of evidence to use against him.

Even the best criminals inadvertently make a mistake and leave a trace of something. Carlos dumb ass just had dumb luck and committed the perfect murder. His prints were at the house but they were supposed to be. A prostitute stole the murder weapon while he was asleep so there was no gun to trace back to him.

Rip watched helplessly as his wife was loaded onto a gurney and wheeled away. The blaring of the sirens meant she was still alive but he had killed enough men to know what body shots from a submachine gun does.

His mind was about as scattered as the army of agents swarming through every room of his house. None of them would ever build a house or furnish it like this so they made sure to be heavy handed during the search. The sound of glass breaking and furniture being overturned didn't bother him in the least. His concern was his lifeless wife who was rushed away. As well as the baby in her belly.

"Nothing," an agent reported to G-money when he returned to the room. He let the dog sniff Rip since he couldn't find a trace of drugs or money.

"Found some cash..." One agent announced and held up a mediocre roll of cash. The few grand was what Rip walked around with but his stash wasn't in the house. He was smart enough to keep his family and his business completely separated.

"Put it in his pocket," G-money shrugged and stood. He headed for the door but stopped just short of exiting. He turned and made eye contact before speaking. "Give up Buddha and you might see daylight before cars fly."

"Who?" Rip asked and spread a smile on the man's face. "The fuck is a Buddha? That fat, green nigga?"

"We'll talk again..." he nodded and stepped from the room. One of the agents pulled him to his feet and escorted him out to the back of a car. He would be taken to the office for questioning but more were on the way.

*****

"He gonna have to buy me some bundles!" the little girl who watched Buddha's cars fussed as she watched his car. Her services weren't really needed since no one would bother his car but it was a good excuse to give the girl money. She had moved on from quarter waters and chips and now wanted bundles and weed.

"Word, I..." her companion began but a convoy of electric company trucks had pulled on each corner of the block. He couldn't see the back side but the building was completely surrounded. There was a brief silence where even the birds stopped chirping. Just before all hell broke out.

"Yoooo!" the girl yelled when masked men filed out of the trucks with machine guns drawn.

One of the lookouts was so shocked he forgot all about his whistle. Agents knew who he was and why he was there so they took him down on their way to the spot. The other lookout blew his whistle fast and furiously until the butt of one of those guns knocked it and a tooth out of his mouth. Twenty agents swooped through the playground, scooping up drugs and drug dealers. A similar scene was playing out in the projects as federal agents swarmed all over Highbridge.

A teen assigned to the laundry went wide eyed with shock as he witnessed what was happening below. He suddenly remembered he was a part of it since he had ten G-packs, ready to resupply the dealers.

"Fuck!" he announced as agents swarmed from both sides. The only way out was the window so he dove face first like Superman. Except, he wasn't so the impact broke a few ribs when he belly flopped on the pavement below.

"Jackpot!" an agent cheered times two when he found the crack as well as the walkie talkie the kid never got to use. That meant Trouble was in trouble since he didn't get the warning above.

"You better, sss, not come, in me!" Keisha moaned when Trouble gripped her ass and dug deeper like he did when he was about to come in her. He needed to change his name to

Lucky since it was the reason he didn't have more kids by her since his pull-out game was nonexistent.

"Ok," he grunted and came in her anyway. His senses suddenly came back to him the second he came.

His head popped up since it was just too quiet. He was still naked when he stepped out on the terrace. His eyes went wide when he saw the chaos below. There was no time to waste since agents began pounding the door with the battering ram.

"Run!" Keisha shouted when she realized what was happening.

"Shit!" he exclaimed and sprang into action. He ran to the end of the terrace and dove under the partition that separated each unit. He scraped his chest and balls on the concrete but didn't slow down. By the time the enforced steel door gave way to see the battering ram he was on the other side of the building.

Trouble was always polite and generous to his neighbors. Which was why he was given clothes and safe haven from the agents swarming all over the building. Keisha managed to get her panties and bra back on before the door came crashing in. She was forced face down and cuffed behind her back as the apartment filled with agents.

"No need for the dog!" an agent laughed when he reached the room filled with coke and crack. They had all kinds of safeguards to prevent this from happening but it happened anyway.

"I don't know what's going on out there..." Tara said she came in from the terrace. Buddha did when he took a look for himself. He heard footsteps in the hall and knew who and what.

"Get down!" he demanded and pulled Tara to the floor. Their bellies just touched the thick shag carpet when the door gave under the pressure. It wasn't reinforced so it gave little resistance.

"Federal agents!" they shouted like they had been shouting all day. The couple locked eyes as they were cuffed with plastic ties.

"Clear! Clear! Clear!" they called as they searched the house and found nothing and no one.

A thorough search of the apartment turned up nothing but they were still carted away with all the others. A total of one hundred people were arrested between the White building and the projects. That meant at least ninety would flip and bite the hands that had been feeding them for years.

Chapter 12

"Where do you wanna start?" an agent asked once they had the Virginia crew lined down the hall of interrogation rooms.

"With the weakest link..." G-money replied and flipped the pictures of perpetrators. He paused ever so slightly at one before continuing. Then backed up to the same picture. His lips twisted and head nodded as he headed inside the room.

"Fucking po-po!" Joey snarled as the man he sold so much coke came in with a badge hanging from his neck.

"You say that like that's a bad thing?" G-money asked, tilting his head curiously. "I'd rather be po-po than a killer."

"I ain't never killed no one!" he proudly proclaimed. He may have spoiled families but he didn't have any blood on his hands.

"I know. That's why I'm coming to you first," he said and paused for it to register. "You're a hustler. A businessman, I get that. A pretty shrewd one gaging how you tapped those bricks. But if you don't play ball with me you're going away forever!"

"Y'all can't give me no life sentence for no damn coke yo!" Joey shot back smugly. Plenty of people they knew caught cases and no one went away for life.

"Son, you sold me a ton of coke over the years! I could have knocked you off after the first sale, but I ran it up on you. This is the feds B. We're gonna charge you for every gram!" the agent reeled.

"Do what you do nigga!" he shrugged and leaned back in the chair.

"Keep that same energy B. Let's see if Buddha is gonna help you now," the agent said and paid close attention. Joey flinched at the name but kept his composure. G-money nodded his way out of the room since he wasn't done with him. It had been a long day so he decided to cut the line and start at the top.

"Sup with my wife yo?" Rip asked subdued when G-money walked into the room. He was joined by the large white agent who liked to rub his balls on people's faces. One look at Rip told him not to try him like that.

"I'm sorry, she coded in the ambulance," he said as he sat.

His partner looked at him, then across at the suspect. Rip was crestfallen as he stared off into space. The case was the last thing on his mind at the moment. A more pressing issue was how was he supposed to carry on without the love of his life. How was he going to live without a heart? G-money waited patiently for him to absorb the grim news before continuing.

"Look, I know you have to raise your kids. So why don't we figure something out," he offered softly. Rip looked up at him so he went on. "Something that will allow you to keep your house. Keep the money you got stashed wherever you got it stashed."

"What are you talking about?" Rip asked, confused. He already knew anything bought with suspected drug money was subject to seizure. Which was why his house was purchased through Jeanine's mother. Buddha taught him how to move money so it couldn't be found, let alone seized.

"I'm talking about a deal. Conspiracy to traffic cocaine. Five years and home with your kids," he offered.

"Sure beats thirty years," the other agent sighed like he had to do thirty. Rip just looked back and forth between the two trying to figure out why they would do him any favors. He was so frazzled from the news of his wife's death he couldn't think.

"Bruh, what the fuck are you talking about?" Rip reeled when he finally figured out where they were going with it.

"Buddha. You do his dirty work while he gets rich. I want him," G-money spelled out. He knew it would be Buddha who could trade up the ladder so he could get the plug.

"Lawyer," Rip sighed, since anything else could be used against him in a court of law. Plus, he knew they didn't have anything on him. He didn't get caught with drugs, money, guns or nothing. The Buddha team was solid so no one would snitch.

"Check," G-money said and stood. "Let's see if your codefendants feel the same..."

"The fuck was that?" the white agent asked the second they stepped from the room. G-money fixed his face to ask what he meant so he explained. "You told him his wife coded? She's in surgery now."

"Well, she did code. They just brought her back," he replied and moved on to the next room. The white agent just shook his head since that was too much for him. He might rub his balls on people's cheek but telling them their loved one was dead was too much.

Howard was in the next room but kept it solid. He was one of the few since most of Jeanine's girls got swept up as well. Everyone of them told everything they knew about her but didn't know much about her man. Bond hearings were two days away which would allow the holdouts to stew for a bit. It wouldn't take long to realize prison isn't the place to be and they would be ready to talk.

"In the meanwhile," G-money announced as he stepped back out into the hall with a statement from Jeanine's ex girlfriend. "I need to shoot up top!"

*****

"We can cut the girls loose?" one of the New York agents suggested. With a hundred people in custody they needed to make some space. They cast a large net through Highbridge and caught a few small fish along with the big ones.

"Absolutely not!" another replied.

They had no evidence of any crime against Tara but would still drag her through the wringer. Keisha was caught in an apartment full of drugs and guns so she might be here for a while. Even the young girls who hung around the young dope boys got caught up in hopes they might have seen or heard something they could use.

"So, we're supposed to sit here twiddling our thumbs waiting for some hot shot?" he shot back.

"Uh, yeah!" the other explained just as the hot shot arrived.

"He's here," the secretary announced when the guest of honor arrived. The local agents felt some kind of way about having to wait to interview their collars but this was his case.

"Gentlemen," G-money greeted as he entered the office. He ran the interstate drug task force so they answered to him.

"We pulled them all. Let us know which one you want to start with and we'll take..." the eager agent suggested. Or at least tried to.

"You'll stand down," G-money cut in and shut him down. "I will interview them all. Can one of you run and get some cheesecake!"

"This mother fucker!" the agent fussed when G-money took the files and walked off. He started at the bottom last time and got nowhere. This time he started from the top.

"A-yo, what the fuck is going on! Where the fuck is my lawyer!" Buddha demanded as soon as the door opened. They weren't provided a phone call like they do on the cop shows but Denise knew what to do once the raid went down. Buddha had a lawyer on retainer for years so he should be there.

"Garrick Craven! My man!" he cheered so jubilantly Buddha had to squint to see if he could see where he knew him from. He couldn't though since G-money always watched from afar.

"I know you from somewhere?" he finally asked.

"Nah, but I know you," he replied and commenced telling him and his wife's whereabouts over the last few years. He had kept close tabs on him but none of it was a crime.

"You should write a book B! Cuz that's straight up fiction!" Buddha howled with laughter. And Buddha should consider acting considering the agent was spot on.

He was the de facto leader of the Buddha crew even if Rip was behind the wheel. He was a fifty/fifty partner in most of the proceeds except the couple extra million Rip earned dealing directly with the connect. "Write one of them street lit books B!"

"Oh yeah, cuz the most prolific urban writer ever came from Highbridge," G-money nodded in a nod to Sa'id Salaam. "Yeah, but no. You're going to prison for a long, long time. Unless..."

"Ain't no unless son!" Buddha shot back before he could even get the foul statement from his mouth. They may have run portions of the Bronx but Giggles ran New York. They could easily swap out a few decades by giving him up but that would never happen.

"I'm saying..." the agent was saying but Buddha only had one word left for him.

"Lawyer!" he announced and formally shut down the interview. G-money knew the cameras were running, now anything he said could be used in a court of law against him. So he pressed his lips together and collected his files.

"Let's see if your lady wants to go home to your kids..." he muttered as he stepped from the room. He went one door over to see what Mrs Craven had to say. From the lack of a case file on her she clearly wasn't about this life.

"Lawyer!" Tara announced as soon as the door began to open. G-money just nodded again and backed out. The next room held the next chick so he entered to try his luck with her.

"Keisha McClure?" G-money read from the chart but made it sound like a question. Once he could get a suspect answering questions he could get somewhere.

"Pssssh!" the young girl hissed and rolled her eyes.

"Look bitch! You were just caught in an apartment containing twenty two kilos of powdered cocaine. Another six kilos of crack cocaine. A handgun, shotgun and semi automatic machine pistol!" he snapped.

"And my fingerprints ain't on none of it," she teased and laughed. Little did he know this girl was raised by Black Rob and Bob. He was barking up the wrong tree.

"No, but I'm willing to bet that the sex stains in the bed will come back to you!" he shot back hotly.

"I'm guilty of having some good, juicy pussy. Lock me up!" Keisha laughed and held her hands up to be cuffed. G-money bit his lip because he would bet she did have some good, juicy pussy. He shook it off and got back to business even if he knew he wouldn't get anything out of her. The best he could do was talk his shit and move along.

"If any of those guns come back with bodies on them I'm going to have you charged with accessory to murder," he hissed and barged from the room. The next room held a nervous looking teen and G-money instantly saw that look in his eyes. That 'I can't do no time, I'm going to snitch on all these niggas' look. "Mr Bam-Bam."

"Naw, just Bam," he corrected since he had dropped the little from his nickname once he reached six feet tall.

"Ok so, let me make sure I got this right?" the agent said and read over the papers in his file. None of them had anything to do with the case since he plucked it from a desk on his way in. "You ran the sales in the projects?"

"Naw, I..."

"That's what Rip said," G-money cut in and flipped a few pages, "Right here. Bam handled sales in University Homes housing projects!"

"He ain't say that!" Bam dared and twisted his lips dubiously. He had known Rip his whole life and would never believe that.

"Said it right here!" he shot back and turned the papers to him. Not long enough for him to make out any of the words before flipping it back and continuing. "How the fuck would I know what goes on up here if your man ain't tell me?"

"I, I..." he stammered but couldn't figure it out. His head shook, mouth opened and out spilled the beans.

Chapter 13

"Craven. Attorney visit," the federal jailer announced and cracked Buddha's cell door.

"About damn time," he grumbled, since jail time is different from regular time. The man was in the Bahamas when Denise reached him but he knew whose money afforded him trips like this so he dropped everything and caught the first thing smoking to New York.

Buddha blinked in the natural light since his eyes had become accustomed to the fluorescent bulbs of the cell he had spent the last twenty four hours in. All the suspects had been isolated to prevent them from talking to anyone else. Even phone calls were denied so no one could communicate about the case. Until the lawyers began to show up, that is since G-money was denying their rights.

"I demand to see my client and the evidence against him right this second!" Alif Shareef demanded. The Palestinian lawyer grew up under Zionist oppression which made him ferocious. He would fight in and out of court for justice.

"There he is right there," G-money announced. He looked totally different in a suite and tie since he planned to attend the various bond hearings.

"You didn't say anything, did you!" the lawyer barked at his client. Buddha twisted his lips into a 'yeah, right' as he was placed into an attorney/client room, without cameras or listening devices that would get cases thrown out of court. They were silent until the guard uncuffed Buddha and left the room.

"The fuck Alif?" Buddha wanted to know since he already knew he was isolated from the business. "I'm clean. Been clean. The apartment was clean. Why did they nab me?"

"That's what I'm going to find out!" he vowed. He also knew the best way to remove a bandage is to just snatch it off so that's what he did. "They made arrest in the Bronx. Long Island and several cities in Virginia."

Buddha just shook his head as he read the long list of potential co defendants. None of them could be linked directly to him since most came on board after he fell back. He knew none of the original crew would flip on him. His face twisted when the lawyer reached the end of the list. He didn't know most of those names on it but the one that was missing stood out the loudest.

"Wait, what about Carlos? My cousin..." he asked as Alif scanned the list once more. The lawyer knew what that meant and gave an ominous head shake.

"There have been over one hundred arrests. I would estimate, seventy will cooperate with authorities," he candidly revealed. "More like, eighty. Eighty five to ninety."

"Well, let's work on bonds. Can we bond everyone out?" Buddha asked like a boss.

"Some. Most, unless there are murder charges..." the lawyer said and scanned the list once again. The more weight they sold the more their bonds would be but so far no one was charged with murder. "But, it's going to be very, very expensive!"

"Yeah, I bet. Get 'em out. Everyone," Buddha sighed and felt his pockets lose weight just that quickly. Alif helped move a lot of his money so he knew how to access it. Meanwhile Alif's cousin was having a similar conversation several hours south.

*****

"Hey Gabriel," Fattah Shareef greeted when he came into the room. He had to repeat himself before Rip even registered his presence. "Hey Gabriel."

"Huh? Oh, sup yo," Rip replied and attempted to slip back into his slump. He had been in a hazy, blue hue of grief since hearing his beloved had died in the shooting. It was a double tragedy since Jeanine was pregnant again.

"I have a bond hearing scheduled for today," he informed but that too barely registered. "There's good news and bad news."

That statement usually prompts people to decide if they wanted the good news first or visa versa. For some the good news served as a cushion for the bad news to follow. Others preferred to get the bad news first so the good news could cheer them up. Rip remained stoic since he had already received the worst possible news. His shoulders shrugged so the lawyer made the choice for him.

"Good news is you didn't sell anyone shit! The case against you is circumstantial at best. A lot of circumstances but still, circumstantial." he spelled out and laid out that cushion. He was going to need it because the bad news was actually pretty ugly.

"Word," Rip nodded. The lawyer had his full attention as he went on.

"The bad news is people have already flipped. Some were calling your name before the handcuffs even clicked.

Even still, most of them never dealt with you directly. More circumstance," Fattah explained.

"What about Carlos and Joey?" Rip asked since they were the only ones who actually did deal directly with him. No one could link him to anything except those two.

"Joseph Smith is..." The lawyer said as he read. His face twisted in confusion but only for a moment since it wasn't hard to figure out. "He's no longer in custody. And Carlos was never arrested."

"Word," Rip sighed and murdered the men in his mind. Not to keep them from testifying but because snitches get stitched where he came from.

"I wouldn't suggest that," his counsel advised as if he could read his mind. "I'm pretty sure I can arrange bail for both you and Mrs Sanchez. Your property will most likely be seized but I'll use my own to secure the bail. I..."

"Wait, what?" Rip winced in confusion. His mother was Miss Sanchez before she married Monte. The only Mrs Sanchez he'd ever met was his grandmother in Puerto Rico and she had nothing to do with the case.

"Mrs Sanchez, your wife?" Fattah asked. Now he was confused at how he had forgotten a whole wife.

"They said she coded," he whispered since the words were too heavy to get much velocity behind them.

"She did, twice. But they managed to bring her back. She lost massive amounts of blood but pulled through. Doctors are optimistic so I want to get her wrist uncuffed while she heals. Her and the baby are going to be ok." he revealed.

114

"Son!" Rip growled and committed yet another murder in his mind. His lawyer read that thought too and quickly shut it down.

"You won't be able to pee in peace once you're out on bond. My advice to you is lay as low as you can possibly lay and let me fight this case!" he insisted. Rip nodded his head but that could mean a lot of things when it came to the notorious RIP.

*****

The lawyers did their job and secured bonds for as many of the defendants as possible. It wasn't possible for those who had already flipped and got released. Still, Buddha and Rip were down a couple million dollars as a result.

To add insult to injury the crew was dismantled and under police scrutiny. No one was going to make any money with the feds watching. Some had plenty of money put up, up and away. But the ball was about to stop bouncing for the ballers. The ones who spent it as soon as they got it. Now they would have to sell some of their jewels and other frivolous shit just to eat.

Rip's first stop as a born again free man was to the hospital to see his wife. He couldn't bear to see his best friend when he was laid up like this but wild horses couldn't keep him from his woman. No best friend, partner, homeboy or other can compete with a man's woman.

"Sup bonita mami," Rip gushed even though Jeanine wasn't looking her prettiest at the moment. Her hair was all over her head and the tube that had been down her throat had her lips dry and ashy. He hadn't even noticed her mother in the chair until she spoke up.

"This is your fault you know," the woman sighed.

"Excuse me?" Rip asked, holding the expletives that should have come with the wild allegation. "My daughter almost died. She did die, twice! Then had federal agents waiting to arrest her the second she opened her eyes. None of this would have happened if she hadn't met you!" she fussed and knocked away a tear.

"You must have forgotten she was wearing boxer shorts and sucking pussy before I came along?" he reminded. The woman actually did forget that phase of her life since it's easy to forget things one doesn't want to remember. There was more so he continued to remind her.

"Forgot she was already in the streets. After getting her ass kicked by her ex boyfriend. Then, I did come along. Now you have two beautiful grandkids! You have..."

Jeanine's mother cut him off when she hopped up and slammed into him. Rip accepted her apology and wrapped his arms around her she could get a good cry. He was right since all that shit happened on her watch. It took a real man to turn her daughter back into a real woman. Then again it always does. Just like a man won't reach his full potential until he has the right woman by his side. It's no coincidence, that's just how God created us.

"How is she?" he asked once she cried herself out for the day. There would be more tears to come but she was done for the day.

"She'll live," she sighed since that was the best part of the prognosis. A bullet nicked the baby but it too would heal.

"Of course. She's strong. Strongest woman I ever met," Rip smiled down at his wife. He knew her friends had already written statements against her and planned to testify for the government. His own lawyer said she was looking at ten to fifteen years if convicted.

The disclosure came with the same warning. The feds were watching, waiting and hoping he would kill them so they could charge him with murder. Carlos and Joey both agreed to testify against him as well but they could easily be impeached. They were hoping he would act so they could get something solid on him.That was just one of many reunions happening at the moment.

*****

"Aaaaaah!" Tara howled as she bust a creamy nut all over her husband's dick. He wasn't far behind her and thrust his hips up until he joined her.

"Fuck!" Buddha shouted as he let one fly. They kissed and writhed in the post climatic bliss for several minutes.

"We need to go to jail more often!" Tara laughed.

"So, you saying Ion knock the boots like that err time?" he dared, knowing better.

"You do daddy!" she purred. The shock of the raid, bust and arrest just made the taste of freedom that much sweeter. The good news was that they were free. He was waiting for a good time to share the bad news.

The feds had nothing on them but didn't let that stop them. They seized their buildings since they were in his and Rip's name. They could eventually get them back but the government just wanted to make it harder on them. Most of their money was hidden but they couldn't get to any of it with all the eyes on them. All the free cash was spent on bailing out the crew. The doorbell rang and their private reunion came to a halt. Not that they minded since it was Denise with the kids.

"Mmhm," Denise laughed when she saw Tara crop all wild on her head.

"Mmhm!" she agreed and laughed as her kids bum rushed her and Buddha. The family enjoyed their time together since no one knew just how much time they had left together.

Chapter 14

"A 'huned and sixty first street," Keisha told the driver as he climbed in the back of a gypsy cab.

"Bet," papi said and hit the door locks so she couldn't run off without paying the fare. Keisha just sucked her teeth since she was wearing jewelry that cost more than the Delta Eighty eight he was pushing.

The car started down the hill on Ogden ave but bust a right instead of a left when they reached the bottom of the hill. She didn't specify the train station on a hundred and sixty first street but didn't tell him to go to Harlem either.

"The fuck you going B!" she demanded and banged on the partition. The shield was bulletproof so her dainty little hand wasn't talking about anything. All she had left was that notoriously sharp tongue so she gave it to him. "Let me out this bitch! I'll have your ass killed! You must not know who my man is!"

The driver stopped at a light on Saint Nicholas and popped the lock. Keisha saw her chance to escape and went for it. It wasn't to be since a man snatched the door open and rushed inside before she could get away. All she had now was her pepper spray so she pulled it.

"Aaaaah!" Keisha screamed as she sprayed.

"Aaaaah!" Trouble screamed when he took a dose in both eyes.

"Fuck!" the driver shouter when the car quickly filled with the obnoxious irritant. He pulled to the curb, blinded and threw it into park. All three piled out of the vehicle, gasping for air and rubbing their eyes.

"Leche!" the driver suggested and tore off into the bodega. He hit the dairy aisle and ripped into a carton of milk. Keisha and Trouble followed and joined him pouring milk into their eyes.

"Y'all gonna pay for that! And mop the floor!" the clerk called from behind the counter. They did both once they got themselves together. Trouble paid the driver and he and Keisha walked hand in hand through Harlem.

"Where have you been!" she fussed and pouted."On the run," he replied and filled her in on his own ordeal. The good people of the White Building provided him refuge while cops and feds scoured the building. He used the terraces to move apartment to apartment when they went door to door.

The feds found all the coke, guns as well as a couple hundred thousand dollars of dope money. His prints were everywhere but luckily for him he had never been arrested so there was nothing to compare them to.

"Well they tried to charge me with all that stuff but the lawyer said not to worry. Then Buddha bailed us all out," she explained.

"Did they search your house?" he asked since she was his stash spot. He had over half a million dollars squirreled away in her closet.

"Nope!" she happily reported. "Now we can go to my grandmother's house down south and leave this shit far behind!"

"Yeah..." Trouble agreed but she didn't buy it.

"Boy, what you got going on?" she pleaded.

"Who?" he asked and got her full lips twisted as an answer. "Nothing ma. Go on down with Trouble. I'm right behind you. Just have to clear up a few loose ends."

*****

"So, now what? I'm free now right?" Carlos asked when he opened the door for G-money.

"Not by a long shot," he laughed as he barged into the house. He tossed a tote bag on the coffee table before taking a seat. Then put his feet on the same table as a show of disrespect.

"Man, you knocked everyone off! Err body out of business!" he pleaded. "That was the deal!

"The deals are not done until the cases go to trial. Trials you're going to testify at. Against Rip and your cousin!" he shot back.

"Buddha ain't even in the game?" Carlos pleaded.

"He is if you say he is!" the agent shot back since he really didn't have anything against him. He might or might not be able to seize assets but he wanted Buddha and Rip behind bars.

"Bruh..." he pleaded again but G-money wasn't hearing it and talked right over him.

"This is your statement," he said and passed him a couple pieces of paper. The two page document was carefully crafted to sink both Rip and Buddha for decades. "Learn it!"

"Man, this is some bull shit!" Carlos moaned as he read the work of fiction. "Killing your sister was some bull shit!" he shot back.

It had only been a hunch but Carlos looked guilty and dropped his head in defeat. The agent thought about killing him right there on his mama's couch but still needed him. He literally shook his head to clear the thought. He would kill him later because he still needed him for now.

"I'ma need some money. Informants 'posed to get paid," Carlos announced and accepted his fate. Plus he had a nasty tricking and smoking habit to maintain. As much money as he made he was close to broke since he fucked it off as quickly as he made it.

"So, get money," G-money replied and kicked the bag over to him before he stood. "I want twenty thousand each!"

"Twenty grand! I was getting them for fifteen!" Carlos complained when he guessed what was in the bag.

"Yeah, until you snitched on the connect," he laughed and headed out of the house. Carlos didn't budge until his car pulled completely out of the driveway and down the block.

He finally moved and pulled the bag closer. A tug on the zipper revealed just a few of the kilos he confiscated over the last few years. Val wouldn't be home for a few hours so he got down to the business of cooking, cutting and bagging cocaine. As soon as he finished he rewarded himself with a nice sizzling rock in his pipe.

*****

Trouble made his way in the shadows just like he was taught by the best. Keisha was safely in South Carolina but he still had work to do in the city. That work started in the projects. A slow, but steady flow of junkies made their way through the courtyard but no one noticed him until he was ready to be noticed.

"Oh shit!" Bam reeled when Trouble seemed to appear out of thin air.

"Sup yo," he greeted and smiled just like he always did when he popped in on his counterpart. The two had become close over the years and it wasn't uncommon for Trouble to come kick it and smoke a blunt. Just like he did now except these weren't usual times since Bam was cooperating with the Feds.

"Cooling yo! You good B?" he asked and stood once he recovered from behind the shock of seeing him. Mainly because he rarely left the projects after the raid.

"Same. You out here grinding yo?" Trouble asked incredibly since the feds just came and chopped the head off the Buddha crew.

"Yeah, I um, had some, I mean picked up a pack from across the bridge. A nigga still gotta eat!" Bam declared.

He was lying though since he was out selling the few ounces he had stashed at a chick's apartment. The lie would allow him to keep whatever he made since nothing was left after the feds swept through. Plus, there was no Buddha crew left to turn the money in to.

"A nigga do gotta eat tho," Trouble agreed and cast a glance up to what he knew was his mentors window. No one was in but he could still feel the man's larger than life presence. "Matter fact, we should shoot over to Sylvia's!"

"Word?" Bam wondered since he never ate at the iconic restaurant. Only because the restaurant didn't come to the projects and he rarely left.

"Word! Let's bounce," Trouble said once the blunt was back in his hand. Now Bam had more incentive to go. Because it doesn't matter how much weed a nigga may have in his pocket he's still going to want to smoke some free weed. Add in some free food and it's a wrap, because niggas do gotta eat.

"Word," he agreed and looked around for someone to pass the work off to since there was a steady flow of customers.

He shook the thought away since he didn't want to have to pay anyone. Instead he followed Trouble over to Ogden where he always parked. It was a short walk from University to Ogden but Bam didn't make it. They were in the middle of the block when Trouble struck.

"Nigga gotta eat," Trouble repeated and lifted the gun.

"Huh?" Bam turned and asked just as he tugged on the trigger. The bullet entered his open mouth which was fitting since he used it to make statements about the Buddha crew. His brains splattered the sidewalk before he fell but Trouble never broke stride. It was going to be a long night.

*****

"We need a new connect," Sampson sighed as he and Delilah rode through Staten Island. He saw the brisk flow of business and knew none of that money would be flowing into his pockets.

"No, we need to chill the fuck out for a while! We just got bailed out or have you forgotten!" she shot back.

Delilah was super hot because her super stupid brother kept kilos in the family house. Carlos implicated them both since he saw her re-up plenty times over the years. The case wouldn't have gone anywhere if they hadn't found drugs in the house.

Luckily Sampson had fucked up all the money he made as soon as he made it so there was nothing to seize. She on the other hand purchased a condo and managed to stock away a million dollars in cash as well as a healthy stock portfolio.

"Well, we're not gonna have to worry about none of that shit! They don't really want us!" Sampson said smugly. "They just want Buddha."

"The same Buddha who just bonded us out!" she quickly remembered. They were already in trouble with their father for dealing in drugs. It would have been even worse was him having to bond them out.

"Yeah, but..."

"Ain't no buts!" Delilah snapped. "You're the one who got busted with fucking drugs in the fucking house! Why would you have drugs in the house!"

"I forgot them," he shrugged and kept on driving. The car went quiet while they both contemplated on their future. Delilah wasn't caught with anything while her dumb ass brother had a kilo and a hundred grand in his dresser. Right next to a gun which would add another ten years to whatever time he got. Time he knew he couldn't do.

"I know where we can get some work," she offered just above a whisper. As distasteful as it was, it needed to be done. "Pull over, let me make a call."

"Bet!" Sampson cheered and swung a reckless maneuver to pull into a gas station. He watched as his sister hopped on the pay phone. She shot out a page and entertained some dude flirting while waiting for a call back.

"Hold that thought..." she said and took the call. Delilah had to turn her back since her brother was staring into her mouth as she spoke. She said what she said and nodded in reply before hanging up and heading back to the car.

"What did he say?" Sampson asked eagerly. He was addicted to tricking and needed money for that.

"We good. Gotta go to the Bronx tho?" she asked since he never wanted to go uptown. Sampson swore the Bronx was dangerous so he sent his sister each week instead.

"Fuck it! Let's ride!" he cheered and pulled back out into traffic.

"You remember when dad used to take us to Bear Mountain back in the day?" Delilah fondly recalled.

"Hell yeah! We used to have a blast!" he shot back with a wide grin. They reminisced over the good times as they traveled borough to borough until they reached the Bronx. They pulled onto Jerome avenue until Delilah spoke up.

"Pull over. Let me use the phone," she suggested and pointed at another pay phone.

"There!" Sampson shrieked, sounding more like their mother than himself.

"Yeah, there," she stressed. He reluctantly pulled in and pulled a pistol from under his seat. She was almost honored that he was ready to buss something to protect his sister, almost.

"Here..." he said and offered her the pistol. She was on her own.

"Thanks bro. Love you," she said and accepted the gun with a kiss on his cheek.Delilah tucked the tool into her purse and headed over to the pay phone. She watched as a dark figure came from the shadows but felt no fear. They shared a nod as he passed and headed for the car. The man pulled his own pistol and tapped on the driver's side window. Sampson looked up just in time to see the flash that closed his case and casket with one blast.Trouble gave her another nod before easing back into the shadows.

Chapter 15

"What the fuck happened!" Giggles demanded as he barged into the hangar bathroom at the airport in New York. Rip knew he could be followed so he didn't dare go uptown to Harlem. He had heard about the raids and was waiting to hear from Rip.

"Shit happened! We got knocked off! Rico charges," Rip shrugged since shit happens. Drug dealing isn't legal and the longer you do it the more you risk getting caught. The trick is to get as much money as you can to pay for the least prison time you can.

"Fuck!" Giggles shouted at the top of his lungs. This would cost millions a month just like that. Not to mention he would have to go back to dealing with Don Chavez himself. The plug had no respect for Giggles and didn't try to hide it. He was a good earner so he dealt with him.

"Yeah, fuck," he agreed since they were indeed fucked. The Buddha crew had a good run but it was officially over.

"You must have a snitch!" Giggles suggested and nodded at the obvious. "Kill everyone who knows your business."

"Already on it," Rip replied since Trouble was still tying up the loose ends in New York. He would have handled the loose ends in Virginia but he couldn't sneeze without agents saying, 'bless you'. The feds were watching his every move. Some were waiting in the terminal now since he had been followed to the airport in Richmond.

"Good, everyone must die!" Giggles said and explained why by shoveling a massive mound of coke up his nostril. More than Rip ever saw anyone consume until Giggles broke his own record when he did the same up the next nostril. "I know that's your man but..."

"But what?" Rip dared. He was unarmed but if he mentioned Buddha's name he would have to try to kill him with his bare hands. Giggles seemed to know it too and kept the name out of his mouth.

"Don't worry about it," he dismissed, so Rip moved on to the next pressing issue.

"We need to let Don Chavez know..." he urged since it was too dangerous not to say anything to the man who seemed to know everything. Drugs were his business so he made it his business to know what was happening.

"We will let him know nothing!" Giggles shouted like Rip was the help. He caught himself before Rip could check him about it. "Apologies hermano. We will figure it out..."

"Si," he sighed. He dapped and hugged Giggles before turning around and leaving the hangar. He would have loved to visit his mother but would return to his wife's bedside. Jeanine was awake and healing but he needed to check in face to face with the man.

"So, what now?" Lupe asked as Giggles watched Rip disappear into the terminal. Unseen agents picked up his tail again and followed him back to Richmond.

"We kill everyone," he repeated and snorted more coke up his nose. "Him, Buddha, everyone..."

*****

"What up yo?" Buddha asked when he took Rip's call. In his mind he could just see agents somewhere in a parked van with headphones on listening to every word. He was partially right though since the call was being recorded but there was no van. Just a computer that captured every word.

"Talked to 'laugh a lot'," he said and paused for his friend to catch his drift. That was the nickname they had given Giggles back when they first met him.

"How'd that go?" Buddha asked and squinted to help see the answer.

"Not good. My mom's and them about to go to the island," he replied and waited again. Neither of them had ever been to Long Island so Buddha caught on.

"Word. Wifey might wanna go too," he nodded in agreement with himself. Things could get dangerous so he needed to move his family to safety.

"Say no more," Rip said since they already said too much. They took it literally and didn't even say goodbye. Instead he sprang into action.

"Pack a bag. Matter fact, don't," Buddha demanded once he hung up from Rip. Just grab the kids and let's bounce!"

"Ok," Tara replied, matching his urgency. She didn't ask where they were going because it didn't matter. Instead of asking questions she rushed down the hall to collect the kids while he went next door to get his mother.

"A-yo! Ma!" Buddha called out as he rushed inside. The living room was empty so he jetted down the hallway. Buddha was moving so fast he couldn't stop himself before barging into the cracked bedroom door.

"You have some good pussy!" Denise's doctor friend had just announced as he crashed into the bedroom.

"That, I did not need to hear!" he groaned and grimaced.

"Or see! Get your ass out of my room boy!" she shrieked while he scrambled to pull the comforter over them. He took a few steps back out of the room and pulled the door up. The barrier allowed him to finish what he came for.

"Ma! You gotta go! I'm sending Tara and the kids down to Puerto Rico with miss Alva!" he demanded through the door. He heard her scrambling for her robe and stomped towards the door.

"What!" she shouted since it wasn't a question. Still, she needed an answer to what he was talking about.

"Look, no time to explain but I need y'all out of the city. ASAP!" he demanded like he was the parent. The roles had somewhat switched once he came of age and became the man of the household. Except now she had a man who had his own house.

"I'm not going to Puerto Rico!" she shrieked. She also saw the determination in his face so she offered a compromise. "I'll go to his house until everything calms down."

"Fine, but now! Y'all can finish that once you get there!" he said and spun on his heels. He was already moving at a good clip but sped up to a full sprint when he heard his kids in the living room. "Where's your mom?"

"Said she was going to pull the car around..." his son was saying but Buddha was out the door while the words were still in the air.

"Shit!" Buddha shouted in midair as he hopped down a flight of stairs in two steps. He twisted his ankle at the bottom but didn't even register. What did register was that he wasn't strapped. It was too late to go back so he kept taking whole flights of stairs in two leaps.

His heart was pounding in his chest when he finally burst through the door to the lobby. A stab of pain nearly dropped him but there was no time for pain so he hopped on one foot. He let out a sigh of relief when he saw his car waiting to pull into a space that someone was pulling out of.

Life went into slow motion mode when a red Jetta whipping up the block came to a sudden stop right next to his car. He was helpless when the passenger and back doors opened. Two gunmen jumped out and lifted matching Mac-10 semi automatic machine pistols.

The guns had been modified to spit fully auto and bursts of gunfire soon lit up the bright day. Everyone else on the block ducked and ran for cover except Buddha who ran straight towards the shooters. Both waved their guns back and forth over the car while firing as if they were water hoses. They saw Buddha when he did a Superman leap as they dipped back into the car.

"Shoot him!" the driver shouted as he pulled away with Buddha clinging to the top of the car. They scrambled to reload while the driver barrelled down the block. Luckily for Buddha he became dislodged by the time they popped in fresh clips. They leaned out and strafed the asphalt before they bent another corner and disappeared.

"You a'ight B?" one of the locals asked as Buddha scrambled to his feet. Well, foot since one was turned at an awkward angle and he couldn't put any weight on it.

"Nah yo! Help me around the corner!" he replied. He leaned on the dude's shoulder and hopped on his good foot back to Ogden avenue. The faces near his car told him all he needed as he approached. Ever the optimist he tried to hold out hope but the flow of blood seeping from the door had killed it. Just as sure as the bullets had killed his wife.

*****

"The fuck you want?" Buddha barked when agent G-money walked into the hospital room.

"Came to check on you. Make sure you good," he said quite unbelievably. "Sorry about your wife."

"Don't be!" he shot back since he didn't want anything from this cop. All he wanted now   was revenge and only he could get that. He recognized the Mac-10s used in the attack since Rip had bought some from Giggles for the crew not long ago.

"Let us handle it. The federal government," G-money offered. "Why catch a murder charge on top of everything else when whoever did this will pay? We know it has to be your connect. Tying up loose ends. Our witnesses have been dropping like flies lately."

"Well, I don't know anything about that," he shrugged since he didn't care if he believed it or not. Trouble got as many as he could before the rest went into hiding or witness protection. His job was done in New York so he headed south to be with his family.

"Your wife is dead," the agent reminded.

"So, what you think I'm about to do a hop bye?" Buddha shot back since his broken foot was in a cast. "Shoot up the block on crutches?"

"I think you feel like you have to handle this yourself. You don't. You're not the plug! You don't run New York. Give me the man who does!" he urged.

"I still don't know what you're talking about," he shrugged and hopped away. His wife was downstairs in the morgue and he had a funeral to plan.

"Keep eyes on him," G-money told an agent as he walked by.

"The fuck he think we been doing?" the man muttered since he had been on Buddha's tail since he bonded out. He even witnessed the shooting that claimed his wife but couldn't do anything to stop it.

"Let ride yo," Buddha told the same agent as he hopped along on his crutches. He recognized the man on a few occasions but seeing him here only confirmed his suspicions. Especially since he already knew the feds were watching.The feds were indeed watching which meant he couldn't clap back now even if his ankle wasn't broken. It was so he would have to wait. His mother and children were safe so he concentrated on the immediate task on hand. For now he had to bury his wife.

*****

"Sup yo," a voice called and spun Buddha on his heels. He recognized the face before he caught the voice.

"How'd you know I was here yo?" Buddha reeled since he had every intention of having a private funeral for his beloved.

"I didn't," Rip replied but that didn't explain his presence. The pain in his voice reduced it to a whisper. The questioning look on his friend's face made him sigh and let it out. "I be coming here to talk to Kita yo."

"My cousin?" Buddha reeled but didn't expect an answer. The better question was,   "Why?"

134

"I cuz I put her here B," he managed because the truth is sometimes hard to get out. The door was open so he got the rest off of his chest. "She smoked that first woolie blunt with me. Then, I treated her like I treated all the rest. I have a lot of blood on my hands B. It's hard to live with sometimes."

"I feel you," Buddha sighed but he really didn't. First, because people have choices. He didn't force Kita to smoke at gunpoint and she was fucking long before he fucked her. But mainly because he had more blood to spill. "Seen cuz?"

"Nah, but heard he's slinging dope from a hotel," Rip revealed. He saw the twinkle in his friend's eye and added the rest to the answer. "Right in front of the police. They waiting for someone to do something to him."

"I bet," he sighed and accepted he would be hard to get to. "Joey?"

"Witness protection. Ain't seen or heard of him yo," Rip said and shook his head. These two were the only ones who could link Buddha to the operations. The feds had no case on either of these two without either of those two.

"Well, I know a guy..." Buddha offered and left it right there. The feds were close but gave him space to bury his wife. "Giggles is mine tho."

"Yeah, and I know just how to get him. Just gotta shake them feds off your ass long enough to pull it off," Rip said and sighed since that was easier said than done. It was a long trip for a long shot that could just as easily get Buddha killed.

"What is Fattah talking about?" Buddha asked, swinging the conversation in a different direction.

"Nothing much. We're good," he replied but Buddha saw through it. Their lawyers were related so he knew it wasn't looking good for Jeanine. All of her girls had flipped on her. Some even had incriminating pictures they turned in. They both could at least get convicted of conspiracy which would land them both in prison. "I got a plan yo!"

"Good!" Buddha sighed because he didn't and court dates were closely approaching.

We Run New York 4

Chapter 16

"The fuck!" Buddha grumbled and slammed down the phone once again. He had been trying to reach Rip all week but couldn't get him on the phone. They had a preliminary hearing scheduled for today so he expected to hear from him before they saw each other at the courtroom.

The weeks since he returned from Virginia had just been a blur in a haze of weed smoke. Buddha usually sat on the same steps in front of the building like he and Rip used to do growing up. He would smoke weed and drink forties with whoever happened along even with the feds watching his every move.

Everyone was on high alert for another attack from Giggles which was exactly why he didn't strike again. He and Buddha were both waiting for things to die down enough to kill each other. Right now he had bigger fish to fry since he couldn't reach Rip. He sprinted to the ringing phone and snatched it up.

"Rip?" he reminded hopefully but got disappointed.

"It's Alif..." his lawyer sighed and Buddha knew right away it wasn't good news.

"What happened yo," he asked and braced himself for what had to be bad news.

"I'm not sure? The prosecutor called me this morning and said Gabriel is taking a deal. Your hearing is canceled?" the attorney asked in hopes his client had some information since his own cousin was being tight lipped about whatever was going on. Cousin or no cousin, Rip's lawyer wasn't saying anything and that could only mean one thing. "He's going to flip on you..."

"Word," Buddha shrugged and lit another blunt. There wasn't time to finish it before court started in the federal building so he just took it with him.

The agents ignored the weed smoke as he got into a car and pulled away. All they could do was pull out behind them and follow him downtown. Buddha was good and high by the time he reached the court house. Alif had the same idea as him and showed up as well enough if their hearing was canceled.

"You reek of weed smoke!" Alif warned as they headed inside.

"Yeah," he giggled since he was beyond giving a fuck. His kids were out of the mainland, his wife was dead and now his best friend was about to flip on him. The fuck would he care about smelling like weed.

"Got any more?" the lawyer whispered since he was going to need a toke or two after this.

"Yeah," he giggled again but luckily it wasn't on him since the dog at the metal detector alerted from the smell. Buddha was searched but released since all the weed was in his clothes and system. The two walked into the courtroom just as it got started.

The courtroom was otherwise clear since the other hearings were canceled or rescheduled. Rip looked behind him when the door opened but turned back around just as quickly. As if he had never met Buddha before in this life or any other for that matter. He and his lawyer huddled one last time before the judge came out.

G-money was sitting behind the prosecutor and didn't look too happy for someone who was about to get what he wanted. He too looked back and rolled his eyes when he saw Buddha come in. He took a seat behind the defense table but only for a moment.

"All rise!" the bailiff announced when the judge stepped from his chambers. He quickly waved everyone down since he never liked people having to stand up for him in the first place. It was a pretentious protocol he could do without if it were up to him.

"You guys lucked out and got the best judge you could have..." Alif whispered as the judge briefly read the legal briefs in front of him.

"Yeah," Buddha replied like that was his word of the day.

"So, I understand the government has agreed to a plea deal?" his honor asked even though that's what he just read. They had to spell it out for the record so the stenographer could preserve it for posterity.

"We have..." the prosecutor said as he briefly stood and sat. He looked over to the defense table since they were up.

Rip let out a deep sigh and stood. He walked over to the stand and placed his hand on the bible. He still wouldn't look at Buddha as he vowed to tell the whole truth and nothing but it. Buddha squinted curiously since he knew he was lying already.

"In your own words..." Fattah prompted and let Rip tell his story.

"My name is Gabriel Sanchez..." Rip began and finally looked at his friend. "I started the Buddha crew back in nineteen ninety. I sold weed until I eventually moved up to cocaine. I controlled most of the crack cocaine sales in the Highbridge section of the Bronx. I linked up with Carlos Johnson from Richmond Virginia and started sending crack there as well. The business took off so I sent my lieutenant, Joseph Smith down to run that part of my operation. I also had my wife introduce me to girls in the strip clubs and had them selling for me as well. She had no idea I was working with her friends. I..."

"No bro," Buddha moaned as he listened to his best friend take the weight of the world on his shoulders. The only person he snitched on was himself as he freed him, Jeanine and everyone else who didn't take deals.

Those deals would now come back to haunt them since they entailed admitting to several crimes. Once Rip finished his spiel the prosecutor asked some cursory questions for the record as well. The case was ready to go back to the judge but someone had to speak now since they couldn't hold their peace.

"Excuse me, your honor?" G-money called and stood. The judge tilted his head curiously since they had no witnesses scheduled for this hearing. The prosecutor could only shake his head but the judge decided to hear him out.

"Who are you?" he asked as G-money stepped from the galley.

"Special agent Gregory Mahoney," he revealed which explained the moniker of G-money. "I ran the interstate taskforce that worked this case for several years."

"Well, congratulations. Good work," the judge offered and tried to continue. Tried to, that is because G-money wasn't finished. "I hear by..."

"Excuse me your honor, but this is bullshit!" he moaned and pointed behind them. "He's the leader of the Buddha crew! His name is Buddha for Christ sake!"

"Your honor, my client's name is Garrick Craven. We have no idea what he's talking about?" Alif said and looked at the prosecutor.

"Uh yes, your honor. The government accepts the plea arrangement," he reiterated. G-money had more protest until the bailiff removed him from the courtroom.

"Forfeiture of real property located on Nelson avenue, Bronx New York. Fine of five hundred thousand dollars..." the judge said as he read from the agreement hashed out by Fattah and the prosecutor. Rip had to agree to it all for it all to work. Even Buddha was smiling until the last line of the deal. "Twenty years to serve in the federal penitentiary."

"No B!" Buddha whined but the gavel came down and sealed the deal.

*****

Buddha kept doing the same thing even after the feds moved on to their next case. He would post up in front of the building drinking and smoking with an Uzi at his feet while waiting for Giggles to make his next move.

Giggles knew it too and wouldn't since he no longer had the element of surprise on his side. Buddha knew he wouldn't make it two feet on that block either so they were at a stalemate. Most of his money was lost but it didn't cost much to do what he was doing. Smoking and drinking his life away.

The deal allowed Jeanine to keep their home and raise their kids. The businesses she and Tara opened all thrived and she was able to hold her husband down as well as the family. Denise made sure to bring Buddha's kids down often so they would grow up together.

Carlos was spared once again and continued to sell drugs for G-money. The agent dismantled more drug crews only to insert his snitches and informants to take over those markets. Buddha was content to smoke his weed and drink his malt liquor as life passed him by.

"You ever had some California pussy my nigga?" a teen asked another teen as they passed by on the steps. Buddha snapped his head in hopes of seeing his friend but it wasn't him. It did remind him of something his friend did say and a light went off.

"The fuck yo!" Buddha fussed at his forty ounce bottle like it was it's fault. It wasn't but he still slammed it on the ground and marched back inside the building. The first stop was next door to see his mother and kids.

"What?" Denise demanded when she saw that determined look on his face as he loved on his children. He had been mentally absent since Tara's death so even they appreciated him being back.

"Who? Nothing," he smiled but she knew that smile as well.

"Mmhm, just be careful," she urged since even she knew Giggles had to die. She often fantasized about walking up to Giggles and shooting him right in his giggler.

"Word," Buddha agreed even though it wasn't up to him. It was a hit or miss, do or die idea but beat a slow death of drinking forties and smoking blunts. Some dudes are on corners and porches dying those same slow deaths in every city in America.

It was something about the way he hugged and kissed his kids that made Denise wonder if she would get to see her son again. He was either going to win big, or die trying and she knew she couldn't stop him if she tried.

All she could do was hug him with all she had before he walked out the door. Buddha had a new purpose when he walked into the apartment next door. He had a couple of guns with his money but knew they couldn't help him with this mission. Trouble offered to come up and help out but Buddha didn't have anything going on for him to help with.

He collected a few grand from around the house and packed a bag. Baggie jeans had been sufficient for sitting in front of the building but he was going a little further today. So he slid into a suite his wife loved to see him in and headed out.

The Bronx passed by the taxis window in a blur but he didn't even notice. The scenery turned into semi suburban Queens once he crossed the Throgs Neck bridge. The scenery barely registered until they reached the busy airport.

"Good luck," the taxi driver said into the rear view mirror. He saw his passenger was deep in thought so he repeated himself. "Good luck!"

"Thanks, I'm going to need it. Definitely a long shot," Buddha sighed. Hearing it out loud almost made him tell the driver to take him back to the Bronx. He would just get some weed, a forty and get his spot on the steps before the kids beat him to them.

"A long shot is better than no shot!" the man replied."Word!" he smiled and nodded. His head tilted back in confidence as he headed through the terminal. He scanned the departure board and saw what he was looking for. The next flight to California was boarding shortly.

Buddha bought a one way ticket just in case he didn't make it back. He watched the ground speed below as he rehearsed his spiel. By the time the plane landed at LAX he decided to just wing it. He didn't have an address to give the cab driver but did have a clue.

"Ben affleck's house yo," Buddha announced as he settled into the backseat.

"You sure you don't want one of them tour buses?" the man turned and asked. The passenger didn't look like the typical Ben affleck groupie but this was a first. Plus the tour buses were a lot cheaper than he would charge.

"Nah B! Just take me there!" he shot back and tossed a couple hundred dollar bills up front.

"Sure thing," the driver shrugged since cash is king. The scenery was exactly what Rip said it was and kept his head swiveling in every direction trying to take it all in. He was almost confused when the car came to a stop in front of a gated mansion.

"Ben Afleck," the driver shrugged.

"Thanks B," Buddha said and got out. He looked through the gate before turning around and headed to the mansion across the street. Rip couldn't give him an address but 'right across the street from Ben afleck' is pretty specific.

Buddha walked up to the intercom and stuck his face in front of the screen. Not that it was necessary since two other cameras had picked him up from the second he stepped from the cab. He reached for the button but didn't make it.

"How can I help you?" a Latino voice asked.

"I'm here to talk to Don Chavez," he said confidently. "Tell him it's Buddha."

Chapter 17

"The infamous Buddha!" Don Chavez announced when Buddha was brought before him. "I've been expecting you!"

"You have?" he reeled. Between the mansion, the party, the naked women and the thorough pat down he endured he wasn't sure what to think.

"Sit..." Don Chavez ordered. The guards who escorted him took the cue and backed out of the room. Buddha complied and sat stiffly on the sofa. "Your friend R.I.P has told me all about you."

"He did?" Buddha asked in awe.

"Yes, and I see he told you about me," he nodded. Rip was told not to but Don expected him to talk to his best friend and business partner. He once had a best friend and partner until he was killed by a rival. Buddha immediately picked up on his demeanor since Rip had adapted many of them.

"So, I guess you know why I'm here?" he asked.

"I make it my business to know everything. I understand eliminating witnesses," Don Chavez nodded in agreement. He knew Buddha had done just that and that's what Giggles intended when he went after him. Still, "I don't condone killing women and children. We don't kill civilians!"

"Well he killed my wife!" Buddha snarled. His scowl deepened when he thought about how much worse it could have been. Bullets had saturated every inch of his car. No one would have survived that attack. "My kids were supposed to be in that car with me."

"And you want permission to kill him?" he asked. Buddha was going to kill Giggles with or without his permission but nodded anyway.

"Yes," Buddha agreed. Don Chavez tilted his head and waited since there had to be more to it. There was and he revealed that Giggles admitted to killing Miguel Camacho. That sealed the deal but Don knew there was still more.

"And?" the plug prodded. The revenge he understood and respected but he saw a familiar glint in Buddha's eyes. There was more to it and they both knew it.

"And, I want to Run New York!" he admitted, then laid out his plan. The plug smiled and nodded as he laid out his plans. From what he knew about Giggles and heard about Buddha this was good for him as well.

"You have my blessings. Handle your business and come back to see me," Don Chavez said and stood. Buddha stood with him and shook his hand. "Would you like to go out to the pool? Enjoy the pool, the women?"

"Thanks, but no thanks. I have work to do," Buddha replied and passed yet another one of his tests. "My driver will take you to my jet," the plug offered and Buddha departed to handle his business. Their business since they would soon be in business together.

*****

"I'll take that," Buddha announced as he stepped from behind the car.

147

"Who are you?" the delivery driver asked since he never saw the man here before. He would know since he delivered here four to five times a week. The lady of the house was obviously very fond of beef and broccoli with a side of shrimp fried rice.

"The man of the house," he replied and tipped him a hundred that canceled the rest of his questions. He had dealt with the last man of the house and he didn't tip him shit. The round lady inside had upgraded as far as he was concerned.

Thanks!" he cheered at his biggest tip of the night. He hurried back to his car to finish the rest of the deliveries. Buddha took the food and rang the bell.

"Coming..." the woman of the house called out but the door was pulled open before she could get to it.

"It's the food mami!" young Herman called behind him. He turned back and looked up at his father and got stuck. Buddha too was confused by the familiar face he was looking down at. He shook his head to focus and saw Jennifer's features come to the front as well.

"Aye dios mio!" Jennifer shrieked when she came through the living room wrapped in a Japanese robe. It came to the middle of her large thighs and gave peeks at her large breast on top.

"Herman go to jour room!"The kid gave Buddha another discriminative glance before running up stairs to his siblings. They all watched from above as the man stepped inside of the house and closed the door behind him. Jennifer lifted her hands to her mouth causing the robe to fall open. She had gained over a hundred pounds since he last saw her naked but still felt a throb in his loins.

"Excuse me!" she finally said and covered her nakedness. "What are you doing here?"

148

"I'm here to free you," he began and paused to let that sink in. The house was a palace but the lack of love made it feel more like a prison.

Giggles very rarely came to see her and the kids. When he did it was usually straight to the basement which was off limits to her. Buddha knew why even if she didn't since her husband shared more with Rip than with her.His visits were scarce but affection was nonexistent. It had been over a year since he last touched her. Even that was a drunken accident since he called her Rosalinda all throughout the act. She stood there blinking which was his cue to continue.

"And to avenge the death of my friend and mentor," he said, lifting his head with the honor that her father admired about him. The honor that saved her honor back in a darkened park in the Bronx many years ago now.

"Giggles killed my father," she asked without the question mark since she knew it in her heart all along. She shuddered at the thought of his touch after he killed her father.

"Yeah and took his spot. Took his crown," he replied. Now the ball was in her court so he waited to see what she would do with it.

"Come eat!" she shouted upstairs to her kids. Little footsteps were heard instantly since they were already watching from the top of the stairs. She grabbed Buddha by his hand and pulled him up the stairs.

"Bente aqi!"There were six bedrooms in the house and Jennifer could have fucked him in anyone of them. Still she pulled him into the bedroom she occasionally shared with her husband. Pushed him onto the side of the bed he slept on when he slept there. The robe fell aside as she scrambled to pull his pants down.

"Fuck!" Buddha groaned when he felt and heard the gag when he reached the back of her throat. He leaned up to watch as the pretty woman performed a spectacular act of oral sex. She licked, sucked, twirled and tugged like a woman possessed. Because she was.

Jennifer didn't suck Buddha's dick for Buddha or even herself for that matter. She sucked his dick for Giggles even if he didn't ever review the security camera footage. She still looked directly at the lens when Buddha began to writhe and moan just before he skeeted down her throat.

She rolled over onto her back and Buddha hopped between her legs. She was so slick and slippery he slipped right inside. He still had to apply pressure since her barely used vagina was good and tight. He had barely made it to the bottom before she came for the first time of the night. Then came again with nearly every stroke. There wouldn't be many strokes since the volcanic vice of a vagina quickly overwhelmed him.

He too did it for Giggles when he pushed to the bottom of her box and exploded. Jennifer kissed his face feverishly as he throbbed inside of her. This could have been a good time to tell him about his son but she let it pass. Young Herman was so enthralled with his father she would have to handle it delicately. Perhaps after the funeral.

*****

"Pssssh," Giggles hissed when he checked his pager.

"Ju wife," Rosalinda teased. She now openly flaunted the fact that she had taken her ex besties husband. She talked absolutely crazy to Jennifer anytime she had to talk to her. They couldn't even play nice anymore which meant their kids didn't get to play together anymore. Which was tragic since they were siblings since Giggles fathered three with her as well.

"Nine, one one," he explained as he reached for the phone. Rosalinda reached for his zipper like she did anytime he had to speak with his wife.

The joke was on her this time since his dick was salty and soft from fucking one of the young mamis on the block before coming home. Plus a hefty snort of coke up each nostril ensured it wasn't getting hard anytime soon.

"Hola papi, can ju come, um..." Jennifer began but got stuck on the word 'home'. Partly because it felt like even less of a home whenever he was here. Another part was the puddles she left on the sheets since Buddha came by quite often over the past few weeks to bang her back out. In between the carefully laid trap they planned. It all came down to this so she gathered herself and pushed the word from her esophagus. "Home?"

"Por que?" he had to wonder why, since he didn't need to drop off any money at the moment. Even he knew she didn't want to see him anymore than he wanted to see her.

"The baby is sick. The car won't start..." she said and laid out a long list of excuses. None should have been needed since this was his family.

"Ok?" he questioned and hung up. He watched Rosalinda for a minute but realized it was futile. Not only had he just bust a nut in the teen on the block but the half gram up each nostril put the dick out of commission for a while. He pulled his flaccid dick from her incinerator hot mouth and tucked it away.

"What are you doing?" Rosalinda asked when he jumped on the computer since he rarely used it. "Nothing!" he shot back with enough venom to shut her down. He wrapped up and headed out to the island to tend to his sick child.

Giggles made record time to his house even after stopping to make calls along the way. He squinted at the nearly new Benz in the driveway and wondered what prevented it from starting. His shoulders shrugged and he continued inside.

Little Herman saw his father pull up and wanted to run out to meet him. Only his mother's stern warning to stay in his room held him in place. Almost since he still cracked the door enough to see and hear.

"Jennifer! Where are you?" Giggles demanded as he barged into his house. He saw the living room and kitchen were empty so he began to march up the stairs.

"Down here..." she called the basement which confused him even more.

"Told this bitch to never come down here..." he grumbled as he descended the stairs. He found his wife had pulled some of the money from the safe and piled it on the pool table. "What the fuck are you doing?"

"It's called a hostile takeover..." Buddha announced as he stepped from the bathroom. He didn't need to point the gun just yet since it made its point dangling by his side.

"Conyo!" he cursed, then laughed. Jennifer and Buddha both squinted curiously since this certainly shouldn't be a laughing matter.

"What is so funny!" Jennifer wanted to know. "Why ju laughing!"

"Because ju a stupid bitch!" he laughed. The sound of even more footsteps made him laugh even harder. Jennifer knew they didn't belong to her kids and turned to the steps as four of the Camacho clan came down as well. The guns in their hands prevented Buddha from raising the one in his hand. Giggles turned to him to explain what was now happening. "I saw the video papi. You fuck my wife better than I do!"

"He always has!" she spat back and took to Buddha's side as the guns came up. One of the men handed him the Desert Eagle Buddha had gifted to Miguel years ago. It was only fitting he killed him with it.

"Yeah, perhaps," Giggles shrugged since he didn't care. "You were a means to an end. I am king and you, you two are dead!"

Buddha didn't try to get a shot off. Instead he puffed his chest and waited to die. Except the gun clicked loudly when he pulled the trigger. Giggles racked the slide to chamber a round but it clicked just as loudly the second time.

"You had one job!" Giggles barked at his man and reached for his gun but he pulled away. Giggles looked confused but soon got his answer when the four guns all turned in his direction. "The fuck?"

"Ju killed my father is the fuck!" Jennifer spat, then literally spat in his face. Meanwhile Buddha relieved him of the gun he gifted to his mentor.

"You killed Javier too!" Javier's cousin snarled and tightened his finger around his trigger. He wanted to pull it but that wasn't part of the plan. This wasn't his kill to make.

"Now it's time for us to say goodbye..." Buddha sang as he slapped a full clip into the gun. Giggles almost got splatted prematurely when he reached into his pocket. Except he came out with a baggie filled with coke. He tilted his whole head back and dumped some of the powder up his nostrils.

"Let's get it!" he demanded and lifted his chin to accept his fate.

"Nuh-uh," Buddha snarled and came closer. He literally growled when he savagely shoved the huge barrel into his mouth. Just like Giggles had done him when they first met. He let out a gag when it reached his larynx.

Buddha tugged on the trigger and nearly took his head clean off his neck. A piercing scream turned all heads towards the stairs. Little Herman was wide eyed with shock from seeing the only father he'd ever known murdered before his eyes. Jennifer took off to tend to him while the men finished up.

"As agreed..." Buddha said and nodded towards the million on the table.

The million was just icing on the cake that made the coup that much sweeter. Giggles being dead was the whole, multi tiered wedding cake. Him being out the way meant they could get back to business the Camacho way.

That put the newly re-minted Jennifer Camacho at the helm of the family business. Buddha would rule with her and Run New York. His first move was murdering the shooters and driver who gunned down his wife.

We Run New York 4

Chapter 18

"Arghh!" Buddha grunted when he bust a nut inside of Jennifer. They had plenty to talk about but he wanted some pussy first. Plus, she wanted him to have some pussy since it coincided with her getting some dick. A fair exchange in any language.

"It's all jours papi!" she reminded just like the old days. Which brought her to the conversation that was long overdue.

"He's mine isn't he?" Buddha asked even though he already knew. Their son looked more like his and Tara's kids than Jennifer's other kids. Now he was able to finally make sense of the vision he had when he came out of the coma.

"Si," she nodded in Spanish, then explained in English. The mention of her mother put a sour taste in her mouth. She felt like Esmeralda knew Giggles killed her father but had no proof. Nothing but a woman's intuition, and that's plenty.

"Is he ok?" Buddha had to ask since the child witnessed the murder.

"No," she answered plainly. Little Herman was a mess and told anyone who would listen that someone called Buddha killed his father. He was old enough to testify so she sent him to Puerto Rico for a while. The while turned into a long while. "Let's let him recover before we tell him the truth?"

"Ok," Buddha agreed. His mother was mainly raising his children since he was busy running New York. They spent a lot of time with Jeanine and Rip's children down in Virginia. He was happy to keep them out of the city and away from the action.

The Black Mob had a toehold in Brooklyn and Queens but Buddha offered them better prices than they were getting and Casper agreed to terms. Which gave him access to some of the Mob's assets, like hitmen. Don Chavez was pleased since some profit was better than no profits.Buddha realized his biggest mistake was expanding down south. This time he concentrated on the city and really did run New York. He had the best seats in the restaurants and clubs. He was treated like a celebrity even by other celebrities and rapped about in rap songs. He never forgot from whence he came and still split all proceeds fifty/fifty with Rip. Not to mention the frequent trips to the   South Carolina prison to visit his partner.

"Earth to Buddha? Are ju there Buddha?" Jennifer sang and laughed as she waved her hand in front of his face.

"Huh? Yeah," he smiled and rejoined her in the room. He had just received a call from Rip asking for a visit asap. "I gotta go see my dude."

"Want I should come?" she asked since she hadn't seen Rip in years now. Not in the years since they reclaimed their city.

"Yeah, you can come on this dick..." he laughed and pulled her on top of him. Being treated like a lady made her abandon over eating and regain most of her figure. She was now a grown woman with kids so he embraced her pouch and cellulite here and there. Grown men always embrace it.

Jennifer was feeling a little rowdy this morning so she spun around and nestled down on the dick backwards. This looked as good as it felt so Buddha propped himself up on some pillows and watched her work. It wasn't long before she coated his dick with that good cream good pussy produces.

She came, he came and then left. The millions they were raking in allowed him to have a private jet on call so he made the call and headed over to JFK. He ran through various scenarios of the urgent visit as he flew south.

Rip had been away ten years now but never asked for anything. In fact, lately he had been declining everything. He would find out soon enough so he settled back and slept for the short flight. Then caught a car service out to the federal penitentiary.

*****

Buddha did a double take when he saw his old friend step through the door the inmates used for visitation. It had only been a few months since he was last here but his friend had changed a lifetime's worth. A large beard framed his face while a crispy white cap adorned his head. He stood for the embrace prisoners were allotted at the start and conclusion of each visit. Any other contact could cause the visit to be terminated.

"As salaamu alaykum," Rip greeted, which in turn explained the physical changes his best friend could see. No matter how close they were, Buddha would never see the internal changes in his heart.

"Word!" Buddha laughed and nodded approvingly. "So, what I'm supposed to call you now?"

"Abdur-Rahman. It means slave of the most Gracious," he answered and explained. That made a lot of sense to Buddha who already knew everyone was a slave to something. Plus he was all for anything that would better a person.

Lots of people they knew went to jail but most came out more fucked up than they went in. Even Trouble developed a heroin habit when his finger prints finally caught up to him. He only served five years but lost himself and his family as a result. Keisha would be there if he got himself together but he would have to get himself together. That's the thing about getting yourself together, you have to do it yourself.

"I told you I was good on money yo," Rip declared once they sat opposite each other.

"Yeah and Jeanine said something too," Buddha agreed.

"And yet, you keep sending more?" Rip chuckled and shook his head. He knew better than anyone on this planet that Buddha was going to do what Buddha was going to do. If Rip hadn't done what he did he too would be wearing a uniform and allotted contact with his loved ones.

"Word," he laughed since that was that about that. "Little man went to rehab. Make one of them prayers y'all be making for him,"

"Word," Rip agreed since he too was rooting for Trouble. The rest of the time was spent switching subjects that ran the gamut from politics, religion and their kids.

"Garrick is getting nice but your Gabby!" Buddha reeled when the talk reached their son's summer league basketball. "You might want a DNA test B."

"Son, I was good at ball too!" Rip declared and got a good laugh out of his friend.

"You sucked yo! Word is bond!" Buddha corrected. It was true that he was the ball player while Rip was the lover. He had finally matured enough to have relationships with all of his kids. The money sure didn't hurt matters either.

"You ever heard anything about them?" Rip asked with mixed emotions.

On one hand he was Muslim now and wanted to let go of his past. He was still from Highbridge though and snitches still needed stitches. What Joey and Carlos did was punishable by death even if he forgave them, he still wouldn't mind hearing about it.

"I got a guy," Buddha shrugged since he outsourced the get back to the Black Mob. They had enough hitters on their payroll to handle it and keep his hands clean. Carlos was still his blood after all. Joey was even closer than family since he picked him to be in his life. Time ran out and they used up their last hug.

Time was running out for a few other people as well...

*****

"That looks like the one right there..." Carlos said and licked his lips at the caramel colored dancer who had locked in on him as well. Maybe because she knew a baller when she saw one. Or it could have a more nefarious motive behind her attraction.

G-money had relocated his chief snitch out to Kansas city. He was quickly getting known around town for his good coke with better prices. The agent decided to keep him around since who slaughters a chicken that lays golden eggs?

Not him, for sure. The super informant was a win/win for him since he was able to sell all the dope he confiscated in different cities. As well as build cases on his competition and get them out the way. Buddha was back on his radar but he would save him for last. Meanwhile the dancer danced her way over to Carlos's table.

160

"Sup lil mama!" he smiled and raised his hand for the waitress.

"Hey yourself," she purred and began to dance at his table. Table dances were ten bucks a song so she was on the clock.

"I ain't seen you in here before?" he asked but it was more of a statement than a question so she just shrugged her shoulders and kept dancing. She did a half turn to let him see her round, little ass since it usually sealed the deal. "You tryna make some money?"

"Duh, that's why I'm dancing," she sniped, shimmied and shook."Nah I mean like, a rack. I'm tryna fuck something!" he cheered as if he scored already.

"A thousand dollars for sex?" she wondered but wasn't sure if that was bad or good. Not that she would but she still agreed."Ok, let's ride," she announced and walked off.

Carlos wondered if she understood the question since girls couldn't just leave whenever they wanted. He got his answer when the new girl returned in street clothes. She was just as sexy fully dressed as she had been in the boy shorts and halter top. A heavy bag was slung over her shoulder.

"Shit..." Carlos cheered again since it sure looked like he was about to score. He held out his elbow and she gladly took up his offer and was escorted out to his car.

"Nice!" the dancer sang since G-money had him riding foreign in the new Benz. It definitely fit his character of a big time dope boy.

"Yeah, a lil something," he bragged and opened the door for her. Not that he had a chivalrous bone in his body. He was just hoping to get a peek under her skirt. She knew it too and made sure to spread her legs wide as she was seated inside. Her freshly shaved box glistened under the streetlight and made getting her home that much more urgent.

"Nice," the girl said again when they reached the nice house he was staying in. It too fit his cover of big time dope boy. She treated him to another crotch shot and grabbed her heavy hand bag as she got out.

He rushed her inside in a rush to get inside of her. The living room, dining room and hall were just a blur when he dragged her back to his bedroom. She lifted her dress overhead and was naked in a flash. Carlos kicked off his shoes, snatched off his pants and draws and dove to the middle of his bed. The dancer climbed up onto the bed but brought the heavy hand bag along with him. He squinted with wonder as she stood over him and dug into the bag.

"Toys?" he asked eagerly since he was with the freaky shit.

"Nope, hammer time!" she giggled as the mini sledge hammer came into view. He looked so confused as she lifted it above her head. He got the point when she swung with a grunt and knocked his jaw loose.

"What-the-fuck-are-you-doing!" he grunted because its hard to talk with a broken jaw.

"Killing you, duh!" she sang and swung again. He lifted his arm to deflect the blow so it got broken instead. He used the other arm for the next blow with the same results.

His legs worked so he rolled off the bed in an attempt to make a run for it. Right plan but the lunatic leaped too with the hammer over her head. She brought it down with all she had, and some she borrowed. It was plenty since the blow caved his skull in. No amount of stitches could fix this snitch. Her work was done but she couldn't help herself.

"Stop...hammer time!" Yolo laughed. She took a twirl under his shower to remove the spray of blood and bone before calling in the kill. Casper had made it a contest since he had another hit man on the other snitch.

"Spot 'em, got em..." Killa smiled through the lens of the scope on the high powered rifle. Joey had just opened wide for a bite of his dinner when the bullet came speeding into his mouth.

The steak was a perfect medium but he wouldn't get to taste it. His brains fell out the massive hole in the back of his head and Killa's work was done. He too picked up a phone to call in the kill.

"Looks like a tie!" Casper announced and gave them both the last target. That too was a competition between the master and the student. Either way this dude was going to die.

Chapter 19

"We should have done this twenty years ago!" Buddha declared when he saw Jennifer in her wedding dress. They had been together since they got back together but it was only Tara's memory that prevented him from taking this step. It was his daughter Denise who urged him to marry her since they were now grown and prepared to leave the house. She didn't want him to be lonely so she gave her blessing.

"Better two decades late than never papi!" Jennifer cooed as she coined a new phrase. Her son Miguel agreed to give her away since Herman still wouldn't speak to her. He may have had Buddha's blood but his personality was all Giggles.

Jennifer sent him to Puerto Rico after he saw Buddha kill Giggles. She hoped he would get over it but he never did and refused to come back to the states. He had a mean streak just like his step dad and honed his dangerous demeanor in the mean and dangerous streets of San Juan.

Unbeknownst to Jennifer he did pop in and out of the mainland from time to time. He would take hits for the Camacho clan but Buddha and Jennifer had long ago turned the reins over to the next generation.

Don Chavez gave his blessings since the money was still rolling in. He even took a private jet out from Cali to witness the nuptials.If Buddha had one regret it was not waiting for Rip, aka Abdur-Rahman to be here. He still had another year or two to go on his sentence but gave his blessings as well.

"Sup yo?" a familiar face smiled as it approached Buddha. Buddha smiled back and threw his arms wide.

"My nigga!" he sighed and squeezed Trouble so hard he grunted. "Where have you been? How have you been?"

"Still down in Carolina," he answered since that part was easy. As for the how he'd been, it was a little more complicated. "Up, down, way down, but I'm up again. Thanks to her and you!"

"Nah, thank her B. All I did was send money," he insisted as Keisha came to collect her hug. "Sup ma?"

"Good!" she squealed and hugged her old friend. She saw the bride and left the men to talk their man talk.

"Good to see you back right again yo," Buddha sighed. He hated seeing his friend struggle with addiction but never made the connection between his own contributions to so many other addicts. Rip did which is what made him visit Kita's grave every night while Jeanine was fighting for her life. It was the catalyst that pushed him to change his life and religion. Because Islam demolished all his previous evil deeds and gave him a fresh start.

"Good to be back with my family!" Trouble smiled as his kids caught up with Buddha and Rip's kids.

"Time to get started..." an attendant advised since, well it was time to get started. Nothing would top Buddha's surprise wedding in the park but Jennifer's idea of getting married in the Metropolitan museum of art was nothing to scoff at.

"Word," Buddha agreed and began to walk up to the altar. Another familiar face stopped him in his tracks as he entered. He turned and walked towards the young man wearing an original replica of his own face at that age. Buddha smiled happily that Herman had come but the young man didn't. "Glad you made it!"

"Me too," Herman said as he pulled the pistol from his waist. The first shot rang out and froze everyone in place. No one here was a stranger to gunshots but it didn't fit in the downtown location. The second shot spurred everyone to action. The attendees all ducked for cover while police and security rushed the shooter.

Herman locked eyes with Buddha as he methodically pumped shot after shot into his torso. He was tackled to the ground and fell right next to his dying father. Buddha still wore that same smile as the light in his eyes went dark.

"Noooooo!" Jennifer screamed hard enough to break hearts. There could be no greater heartbreak of a son killing his own father on the day he was to marry his mother. "Why Herman! Why!"

"He killed my father!" Herman said proudly as he was cuffed by the cops. Jennifer only cried harder as she finally made the revelation she should have made a long time ago.

"No nino, he was jour father..." Jennifer wailed as her first born was carted away by the police.

*****

Buddha's funeral was a star studded affair. The superstar dope boy was sent off in ghetto fabulous style. A horse drawn carriage carried his fancy casket through the streets of Highbridge. They even swung through the projects one last time before heading across the bridge to Harlem.

The church sold tickets for standing room only event. His mother and children shared the front pew with local politicians and celebrities. An R&B group with the number one song in the country sang gospel songs before the congressman gave the eulogy. The least he could do after Buddha helped him get into office. He was in the middle of his spiel when all heads and eyes turned to the back to see who the latecomer was. He had to be somebody to be let in the standing room only church.

"Who is that?" a lady lucky enough to get in asked.

"Ion know?" her friend replied and squinted to see if it would help her make him out.

Some had never seen him before while others hadn't seen him in nearly twenty years. Plus Rip didn't look anything like he did before. Gone were the fancy clothes and no jewels on his neck, fingers, ears and wrist.

Even his rich nigga swagger was replaced by a humble demeanor that match the long beard and fresh, white kufi on his head. The old Rip would have had a fly girl on each arm. This one had a prison guard flanking him. They removed the ankle chains but his hands were cuffed in front of him. One funeral goer in the back knew exactly who he was.

"My man Rip," G-money mumbled under his breath. He proved hard to kill since he was still a fed. He had been all over the country and world busting drug dealers while dealing drugs of his own.

"Papi!" Rip's daughter Gabriella moaned and alerted her siblings and mother to his presence. The eulogy was paused as all of his kids lined up to hug him. Next was Rip's kids and finally his faithful wife. Once the reunion was complete he was seated and the congressman continued.

The procession proceeded to the cemetery and Buddha's final resting place. More words were said before the casket was lowered into the ground. He was the glue between so many people that they said there last goodbyes, knowing they would probably never see each other ever again.

Rip said his 'see you laters' to his wife, kids, niece and nephew before being taken away by the guards. He would be in a halfway house next year and home a year after that. He and Don Chavez gave a respectful nod as he passed. The plug actually gave a slight bow to the stand up guy.

"Hold..." One of the guards demanded as a man approached. He kept on coming and raised his badge.

"Federal agent," G-money announced and showed them his credentials. Rip furrowed his brow and wondered what the man wanted. He found out when he stretched his hand and spoke. "I respect what you did. I've been at this for thirty years and I've never seen that before!"

"Tuh!" Rip huffed and spit in his palm. The guards pulled him away and hustled him into the car.

"Word up B!" G-money laughed and used the saliva to slick down his waves. He was all smiles when he walked back to his car. He wasn't the only one smiling since he had parked at a distance to snap a few pictures of the mourners.

"Ready... set..." Yolo sang and Killa joined her at, "Go!"

Both pressed the red buttons on the boxes they held in their hands. Time healed their wounds and they were now working together. The red buttons detonated the matching bombs they placed in and under his car.The bomb inside splattered G-money all over the interior. The second bomb flipped the car over and set it on fire. And that was the end of G-money and We Run New York.

The End

Epilogue

"Uncle Buddha was the illest!" Gabriella moaned. She and her siblings along with Buddha's kids had met after the funeral to kick it and reminisce.

"Word!" Bullet cheered and lifted his soda for a toast. Rip's youngest son was named Richard but the prenatal bullet he took left a scar on his cheek and gave him his nickname.

"Word!" Buddha's oldest son Garrick toasted as Gabriella rubbed his foot under the table. They were raised as cousins but as they both got older and finer they were losing track of that.

Garrick was the splitting image of his handsome father. Actually nearly identical to the older brother he only saw once, when he killed their father. He inherited his sharp business acumen and hustle as well. The old timers liked to call him little Buddha but he shunned the moniker in favor of his own identity. He wanted to go by G-money but uncle Rip lost his damn mind and shut that down. Now he just went by G.

Rip's son Gabriel went by Gabby and favored his mother more than father but the personality was all Rip. He had become the man of the house at twelve since his father was away. Life in Virginia sheltered Rip's kids with Jeanine but he spent all his summers in the Bronx and developed a

Highbridge swag like his father. The stories they heard about their famous fathers mesmerized the older sons. They may not have wanted to be their fathers but wanted to be bosses just like them.

"I'm just ready to go to Atlanta!" Denise sang. She and Gabriella had chosen Spellman college over all the other schools they had been accepted to.

"Word!" Gabriella cheered and high fived her over the table while still rubbing G's leg under the table. She was called Gabby too so people had to specify girl Gabby or boy Gabby.

"Ion know about y'all two in Atlanta by y'all selves!" Bullet protested. He may have been the youngest but by far the most outspoken.

"Word..." G agreed and looked at Gabriella. He had no idea what to do with her, if anything but wasn't ready for her to be that far away from him.

"Shit, I'm going too!" boy Gabby decided. He had gotten through high school with flying colors but had no desire to go to college. Same with G who could have played collegiate ball anywhere he wanted.

"Atlanta huh?" G asked and looked at Gabriella. She smiled and nodded her vote.

"We are not just going to Atlanta..." Bullet decided. Nope, he had bigger plans. "We're gonna run Atlanta!"

We Run Atlanta, coming up next!

In the meantime, check out an excerpt from Love, Lies and Lace fronts.....

Loves, Lies & Lacefronts

A Southern Love Story

A Novel By

Sa'id Salaam

Chapter 1

"Girl, let me see what he working with!" Shandera fussed as she took Bella's phone out of her hand. The animated woman was always fussing whether she was happy or sad, melancholy or mad. Part of her theatrics were a frown, grimace or twisted lip at whatever was going on at the moment.

At this moment, they were discussing Bella's latest suitor; well, his dick, anyway. There were plenty of conversations at Bella's beauty salon but most had something to do with somebody's dick. Even a conversation about the pastor's latest sermon would somehow get a dick in it. Food, dick. The weather, dick. Music, dick. Dick, dick, dick the long day through.

"Damn, girl!" Bella complained about her snatching her phone away. She may have been the boss but most times, she was one of the girls. She put a hand on her shapely hip and batted her greyish eyes in mock protest. Technically, her French, Indian and African American mix made the girl a mutt, but it came together to form an exotic beauty that turned heads everywhere she went. She couldn't keep a man, though, which explained the new dick pic in her phone.

"I know that's right! I needs to see the dick up front!" Alexis huffed. The big woman was fronting, though, because she couldn't take any dick anyway. The average six-inch variety would have her whooping and hollering like an Indian on the warpath.

"It's the little dicks you gotta look out for! All four of my baby daddies got little dicks," a customer added from Shandera's chair.

The hairdresser stayed in hot demand due to her skills and vibrant personality. She was a name brand to be dropped, like Prada or Gucci. She only played second fiddle to Bella, who was widely regarded as the best hairdresser in the city, if not state, East of the mighty Mississippi, have her tell it. There was a rivalry right beneath the epidermis of their friendship but it was to be expected since every Jesus needs a Judas. It's the cost one paid to be the boss. And being the boss meant you just had to stay on guard for the inevitable cross.

"Eh, it's okay. No bumps or bruises. Nice curve, good veins," Shandera said as she analyzed the prospective penis. She turned and twisted the phone to view the dick from different angles. The woman was an expert after all when it came to dicks. A dick-ologist, if you will. "Seven, maybe eight inches. If he know how to work it, you may be in business."

"Chile, let me see this thang!" Sherbert, the resident sissy, hissed like sissies do.

He then rubbed his big hands on his apron and came over to inspect. "Mm-hm...un-huh...I know him! Dennis McDaniels, age 32, lives at 25 Lafayette Court in the 7th Ward."

All mouths gaped at the news, except for Bella, that is. She just shook her head and laughed. The girls often sicced the sissy on any guy they thought about getting serious with. A sad fact was that a lot of the men out there would fuck with a man if they could get away with it. Only the owner of this particular penis wasn't named Dennis and he wasn't from 7th Ward.

"Eeehh! Wrong answer!" Bella buzzed like a game show. "That ain't him and he ain't from here!"

That was all they were getting out of her about her long-distance lover. They were still cultivating each other after meeting on social media a few months ago. The subject finally got around to sex, hence the dick pic. Most dudes will shoot one off in a second to a woman's inbox. Not Gavin. No; he took it slow.

"But, how you know that's really his? Dudes catfish dicks, you know," Alexis threw in, and she was right. Some will catfish a whole body and photoshop their head on it. Yes, it's deceptive, but so are contacts and lace fronts. Those may not be his pecs or abs, but some women don't look nothing like their pictures, either. Many a man have taken a woman home only to wake up to another one."

"Girl, what kind of man would have pictures of another man's penis in his phone?" Bella demanded to know in a WTF tone.

"Um…right here, Chile!" Sherbert raised a hand and waved.

The whole shop cracked up and cackled in laughter. No matter how miserable life could be on the outside, the shop was always good for a laugh. There were plenty of tears as well.

"My point exactly," Bella cosigned.

"Oh yeah, Sherbert, what's up with ole boy I asked you about?" Baby Girl asked hopefully. The nineteen-year-old had just completed cosmetology school and landed her job at the hottest salon in New Orleans. The job was part luck, part charity since Bella knew her mother from around The Ward. Her story was similar to her own, so she had to show love.

Angelique's mother, Demetria, had her at fourteen, by sixteen she was using dope, and was dead by seventeen, leaving her baby girl behind. The whole hood adopted the baby and dubbed her Baby Girl. The hood stood up and got her through high school and then cosmetology school. Baby Girl had a penchant for the bad boys she grew up around. Luckily for her, she had Sherbert and the rest of the gang to school her on them.

"Who, Slugga? He gay!" he nodded in agreement as he whipped out his phone with the proof. They always wanted proof when it was a dude they really liked. Even though sometimes that didn't stop some if they really, really liked a guy. It was one of the reasons the HIV rate was so high in the city. Another was the constant tourism that helped diseases flow to and fro, far and wide. People came for Mardi Gras and left with a lot more than beads. In the city's defense, plenty of those tourists arrived with diseases of their own, trading STDs like baseball cards.

"Damn shame!" Baby girl fumed, seeing the goon with dreads and gold teeth butt-naked in the sissy's phone. His jailhouse fine frame was covered in crude tats, adding to his ghetto appeal. He was gay, though, so, "You can have him."

"I already did! You can get him back," Sherbert laughed twice, once at his little joke and again at the look of utter disgust on the young girl's face. It was exactly the reaction she should have had.

She made a big production out of deleting his number from her phone and him from her life. Bella nodded her head in approval, as it was the reaction she expected. She couldn't watch the girl forever. She may own the hottest salon in the city, but she was making plans to leave.

"Girl, how you end up with a building in the French Quarter anyway?" a newer patron asked, knowing that the buildings in the gentrified city were worth millions and Bella was barely thirty.

"Oh boy!" Shandera groaned playfully even though she was serious. She had heard the story about Bella's grandmother a hundred times already. This would make a hundred and one as Bella fondly recalled the come up of the woman who raised her.

Chapter 2

"My Grandma was a bad bitch back before bitches was supposed to be bad. A hustler fo' real…"

"Monsieur Beufonte, the new cook is here," the maid announced with a timbre of fear in her voice. She should be scared, after what happened with the last cook. The one who got chased out of the estate with a butcher knife in her back and her panties at her ankles.

"Let me see her!" Mrs. Beufonte insisted, rushing ahead of her husband since he was the problem. She'd walked in on her husband and the last cook having oral sex in the pantry. She'd specifically requested a black woman this time, hoping that would keep his dick out of her. Her racist French husband certainly wouldn't stoop that low, or so she thought.

Mr. Beufonte followed behind her stoically. Business was good here in New Orleans but what he loved most about America was the loose women. All of his rich aristocrat friends regularly had sex with the help. While France was known as the country of romance, they were fucking over here in the United States. He had no use for the black servants most of the city's elite families used but loved all the white trash the Deep South had to offer.

With a name like Bella, both the Beufontes were expecting a big black woman in a white dress with a rag wrapped around her head. They thought they'd have to train her in the fine art of French cooking, just like the last one. Both were shocked, however, when they actually saw Bella. She was black, alright, but the only thing fat on her was concealed in her panties. The tight white dress snitched on the roundness of her ass and flatness of her chest.

"Perfect!" Mrs. Beufonte cheered and cracked up at the woman, knowing her husband wouldn't touch her. She was so busy laughing at her black skin that she missed how smooth it was. Nor did she catch how it contrasted with her dark grey eyes that produced a seductive look about her. However, what she did notice was her thick black hair. It was done in big bouncy curls that shined in the Louisiana sun.

"Gal, who did that to your hair?" Mrs. Beufonte demanded, as if she had done something wrong.

"Never mind her hair. Can she cook French food?" Mr. wanted to know. "I do not eat this, this garbage they eat over here!"

"Funny, because didn't I walk in on you eating garbage in the pantry?" she shot back. The help ducked their heads to conceal their mirth.

That was enough to send him rushing red-faced from the room. All eyes shot to Bella who lifted her head like a person who liked attention.

"Well, to answer yo' questions, I shole can cook French food. My mama cooked for a French family for thirty-years. Twenty with me right by her side and taught me everything she knowed," she replied proudly.

Her mother had cooked and cleaned herself to death for other people, dying without a dime. Bella vowed she'd never live or die like her mother. She socked away every extra coin she earned to one day have her own. Her own beauty salon, that is, because cooking was just a means to an end.

"And, your hair?" Mrs. asked once more. She fully intended to hire whoever did the black girl's hair. If someone could turn nappy black hair into bouncy curls then they would work wonders with her luscious blonde locks.

"I did it myself," Bella replied, lifting her chin even higher in pride. "I'm also a beautician!"

"More like a magician than beautician. You turned nappy copper into smooth silk," the woman of the house said, offending Bella for a second time. Bella had a three strike rule like in baseball, except she would fuck your man upon the third infraction.

"My mama was Indian!" she huffed indignantly in explanation of her sinuous hair, a battle she'd fought her whole life in her native 7th Ward.

"Did she put a spell on your nappy hair to make it like that?" she asked for strike three. "Can you do my hair?"

"I'm here to cook! Now, if you want to hire me on my off time, that'll be just fine."

"Fine," Mrs. Beufonte huffed in agreement. "I'll give you five whole dollars to do my hair, if you make it look just like yours."

"No, you won't. I charges ten, whole, dollars to do hair," Bella insisted. She knew her worth in the kitchen, bedroom and salon. Some days she would work all three, only to sock all the money away. Rent for her half of the duplex shotgun house wasn't much so the rest got saved to purchase her dream.

"Fine, ten dollars then!" Mrs. huffed, like she had a choice. She didn't because, again, Bella knew her worth.

Bella did the woman's hair and she was soon the envy of all the socialites. She paid top dollar to stunt on her friends. Her worth was about to go up...

*****

"Police chasing Slugga dem through the square!" Hustle-Man announced as he walked in. The booster, import/export, wholesale retailer always had the latest everything in everyone's sizes.

"Oh no!" Baby girl fussed and ran to the window just as Slugga blew past in a stolen Volvo. He was blowing a blunt of loud and laughing even louder as he ran from the police.

"Didn't he just say that boy was gay?" Shandera demanded, scrunching up her pretty face.

"Chile, they don't care. You know how many gals I gotta fight 'bout they man!" Sherbert said, shaking his head.

"Anyway, what you got for us today?" Bella turned to Hustle-Man and asked. She had plenty of money but wasn't above saving some cool cash buying the hot goods.

"What don't I got?" he shot back. The tall, handsome man was the perfect salesman. He could work at any of the city's elite dealerships and get rich, but he was addicted to the streets and the city's drug of choice; heroin. He was a functioning junkie who kept up his appearance. There was another junkie just like him who worked in the salon. One of its beautiful beauticians was also a junkie.

The women, along with Sherbert, gathered around and perused the merchandise. Hustle-Man sold Fire Sticks, DVDs of the latest Hollywood movies and porn, shirts, shoes, watches and maxi pads. By the time he left, his bag was empty and his pockets were full. Time to see the dope man.

"I'm gonna wear these on my date tonight," Bella announced, holding a pair of earrings up to her ears.

"Thought you had a long-distance boo?" Shandera pried like she always did. For some reason, she needed an explanation for everything everyone did.

"I do, but he long-distance," she laughed. "A bitch still gotta eat!"

URBAN AESOP PUBLICATIONS

Presents

DAWGS

a novel by

Sa'id Salaam

Dedication

Dedicated to Tisha Andrews. Too often we dedicate to the dead and overlook the living. I want to acknowledge one of my closest friends for your friendship. Thank you.

Seven high tech electric bikes caused all heads to turn as they whipped through the Manhattan streets. The riders all wore colorful, leather riding suits that matched their bikes and helmets. A turbine whine replaced the usually obnoxious roar of motorcycles but still added some cool to the hot and muggy summer night.

The riders scanned the lines of pretty people in front of the many nightclubs catering to the many fetishes of the city that never slept. Slick hair and gold chains lined a mainly Italian club while droves of multi shaded people waited to enter the hip hop club.

Anyone of them would have sufficed but they were headed to the Meet Market. A semi underground club that catered to their kind. Most people would drive or walk right past the venue without knowing it was even there. Those in the know just followed their nose to the hottest spot in the city. In any city since they were popping up everywhere.

The leader of the pack rode slightly ahead while the others rode two abreast behind him. He lifted the blacked out visor of the helmet and inhaled all the aromas that made up New York city. Curry mixed with arroz con pollo, baklava, gunpowder and good weed. Through it all he smelled his favorite meal loud and clear. A glance up to the sky showed a full moon in all its glory.

The lead rider pulled in front of their destination and backed his bike against the curb. He was indeed the leader so his followers followed suit and parked. They removed their helmets, putting their rugged good looks on display.

Rajeem stood a solid six foot one and had the build of an action figure. His complexion fell right in the middle of the race spectrum despite his classic African features. The high cheek bones of eastern Africa accentuated the thick lips of at least part of his ancestry. Bright, almost yellow skin gave a hint to the other part. His wavy hair had a brownish hue and flowed into a tapered beard.

"Smell that?" his sidekick Dog asked as he kicked his kickstand. He pulled his helmet off and sniffed the air.

"Yeah," Rajeem said quickly. He had actually felt it, before he smelled it. The mood of the pack darkened when a Benz with darkened windows pulled to a stop across the street. No one needed x-ray vision to see since they could smell their foes before they opened the door.

"Let's eat these clowns!" Beans asked as he unzipped his leather. He was the hothead of the pack of hotheads but Rajeem showed some restraint, for once since he was always down to ride on his enemies. Maintaining the alpha male spot took frequent acts of extreme violence.

"Some other time," he said and snarled at the men as they approached. Tonight was about satisfying another appetite so it could wait. He joined his pack in glaring at their enemies.

"Not enough, you need more people," one of the men from the Benz bragged. Lycans could be arrogant like that since they were slightly higher on the food chain.

"Some other time," Rajeem repeated and turned to enter the club with his pack on his heels.

The club may not have had a sign out front but was still filled to the gills inside. The mixed race, income and species club catered to the discreet of different breeds. This was one of the few places on the planet where they all coexisted.

The leader led the way up to the VIP section reserved for alpha males like himself. A lessor pack abandoned a table when they saw him approaching. The easy way always beats the hard way so they took it.

"Drinks on me!" Rajeem announced and tossed a stack of hundreds in the air. It was similar to tossing bread crumbs to the pigeons in Lincoln Park. With similar results, since a small flock of birds came rushing over.

Rajeem and his pack made a scene running through bottles of bubbly even though alcohol didn't have any effect or affect on them. It did have quite an effect on the women who liked that sort of thing. Money has a magnetic pull that draws women like birds to bird feed.

"I'm Shontay!" the lead pigeon introduced to Rajeem once she ascertained he was their leader. She always got the head of whatever crew and left the leftovers for her girls. Just like the lead groupie gets the lead singer while her friends settle for hype men, sidekicks and security.

"Rajeem," he replied and took her hand. He offered an old school kiss on her hand even though he was as far from a gentleman as Mecca is to Las Vegas. Figuratively and literally. His mouth salivated from the smell and taste of a woman.

Rajeem and Shontay engaged in verbal foreplay as he felt her up like one does a melon in the market. She was as plump and firm as any ripe fruit should be. He reached under her tight tube dress and inserted a finger into her vagina. She showed off and gave it a squeeze. Once he got his finger back he took a sip of the juice and knew she would be some good eating. Meanwhile his crew shared mean mugs and snarls with the Lycans across the bar.

Lycans were a superior being to werewolves since they were harder to kill. In even numbers they were too much for a werewolf. They were generally stronger, smarter and more calculating. They could easily kill werewolves with a silver stake or sword through the heart. They evolved with the times and now carried silver bullets in the high tech weapons they produced.

Lycans could be killed as well but it took a separation of the spines to do it. It was that advantage that made the Lycans in attendance snarl arrogantly. They too were on a mission since the Meet Market had the best meat in the city.

"I'm out," Rajeem announced and stood. Shontay stood and wobbled from all the champagne she had consumed. The liquor served as a brine or good marinade would do.

"See you back at the spot," Dog said to his departing back and turned back to their foes. The Lycans had shifted their interest to a couple of big breasted white girls. Alcohol had no effect on them either but turned the white girls red like ripe lobsters. Fitting since the Lycans planned to eat them.

Lycans were usually more reserved than the wild werewolves. They knew their survival depended on staying off the radar. As long as they didn't make a mess they could pull it off without their leader finding out. Especially since he was all the way on another continent while they scouted this new city.

"Ooh I love to ride!" Shontay cheered when Rajeem escorted her to his bike. She giggled cleverly at her own double entendre and mounted the bike behind him.

"Is that right," he said as he passed her his helmet and helped her put it on. The electric engine whirled to life when he hit the ignition. She wrapped her arms around his torso and held on while he turned the city sights into a blur.

"Mmhm," She moaned and rocked against the vibration of the engine seeping through the seat.

When they reached the Lower East side Rajeem hit a button on the bike that opened a large door of a loft building. The door opened into an elevator and he rolled straight on. He hit the same button to close the door behind them. He hit the top button on the elevator panel and rode up to the top floor. The elevator door opened right into his living room.

Shontay almost came instantly when she saw how he was living. Most of the industrial decor would have to be admired some other time since he carried her straight over to the overhead loft where his bed was perched. A remote caused the blinds to roll up and flood the area with moonlight.

Rajeem sat her down and put on a show of coming out of his leather riding suit. Under the jacket was a fitted T-shirt that displayed his well defined body. He peeled it off and Shontay fixated her eyes on his abs. She reached out and ran her manicured nails over them like a washboard. Then came the dick.

"Oh my!" She marveled at the wood in front of her.

"So much for that myth about light skin dudes huh?" Rajeem laughed. Shontay just leaned in and gave it a kiss. She soon had a mouthful and went to work. The woman ran through a medley of her repertoire of head techniques. She had more tricks in her bag than Felix the cat but only made it halfway before Rajeem pulled out of her mouth and pulled the dress over her head.

"Uh, you gotta eat me first!" she protested playfully. She was batting around 500 with the demand. Most men regarding going down on a one night stand like eating food off the ground. The gritty, grey concrete sidewalks of New York ground at that.

"I'm going to eat you afterwards," he offered in compromise. That would be a first, but better than nothing.

She began to lay back but Rajeem had other plans. He reached down and flipped her over onto her hands and knees.

"I love doggy style!" she proclaimed and put a mean arch in her back.

"More like wolfie style," Rajeem laughed at his own joke as he fondled her box until it soaked his fingers. The juice box was no laughing matter so he leaned back and eased inside.

"I, like, wolfie style!" Shontay managed between firm thrust that tapped on her cervix with each down stroke. Rajeem just nodded since most did even if most didn't get to tell anyone about it afterwards. The pounding that followed sounded like a round of applause as the slap of skin echoed throughout the large loft. Soon her body shivered and shook as an orgasm pulsed through her body.

Lots of men change once they get the pussy, but Rajeem began to change while he was still in it. Shontay noticed the increase in length and girth inside of her. She felt the grip on her hips change sharply as his hands changed to paws with claws. The attempt to pull away only caused the claws to sink into her skin.

"You're hurting me!" she protested. Her pleas fell on deaf ears because Rajeem's ears were growing long. His beard spread until it met the hair on his head, covering his entire face with hair.

The crunch of bone and tendons joined her screams and filled the air as the man transformed to beast. She soon had a full fledged werewolf inside of her. Putting an end to her 'all men are dogs' narrative. This one was a wolf.

Shontay's shouts and screams were sure to wake the neighbors, had there been any. However Rajeem bought the whole building for privacy. Her wails were nothing compared to the sound of the half man/ half wolf reaching a climax of his own.

He leaned back and let out a howl that could be heard for miles. Dogs cowered in dog houses or under beds when they heard it. Shontay tried to scramble away but Rajeem intended to keep his word. He said he would eat her after and eat her he did.

"No!" The terrified woman screamed at the top of her lungs when she saw the beast behind her. An attempt to escape was thwarted by his strong grip.

She wasted another prize scream when his teeth sank into her hindquarters. Predators often start there to prevent their prey from escaping. A satisfying rush of hot blood filled his mouth and fueled his feeding frenzy. Rajeem literally devoured the woman right there on the spot.

This wasn't the only bloodletting in the city. Across town his pack was doing exactly what he told them not to do.

*****

"Is it some other time now?" Beans asked when he saw the Lycans escort their own prey out of the club. He sounded like an exasperated toddler impatiently stalking a snack his mother told him to wait for.

"Bruh," Dog said, shaking his head. He knew there was no talking him down so he stood and followed him as he followed them. He could be the difference that would swing the massacre one way or the other. The driver and passenger split up getting into the front and back seats with one girl apiece.

The six remaining bikes pulled out after the Benz and followed from a distance. Their extraordinary sense of hearing and smell substituted the need to keep eyes on the vehicle. They followed the scent of their prey from blocks away. They all pulled in separate directions and followed their noses.

The Lycans possessed the same powers of sight, smell, hearing, touch and taste but were preoccupied with the feel of tonsils on the tips of their dicks. They guided the blonde heads up and down ignoring the danger lagging close behind. They were under strict orders not to prey on people without permission. The Lycans usually fed on sheep and other farm animals but nothing tastes as tasty as humans. Eating people could be messy in more ways than one. This is why their leader strictly forbids it unless given the order.

Missing persons created missing persons reports, and investigations that could shed light on their existence. They were hard to kill but not impossible. Human hunters could be dangerous if they caught wind of them. The boss wasn't here now so they decided to break the rules. It was only dangerous if they got caught.

"Here," the passenger in the back seat announced when they reached the hood side of Central Park. The driver responded by pulling over and turning the car off.

"Wolves," the driver said and sniffed the night air as they stepped out of the vehicle.

"So? They don't want these problems," the passenger laughed. There was generally a precarious coexistence between Lycans and werewolves. The occasional clash usually resulted in dead werewolves since the Lycans were deadlier. Sometimes it could go the other way when they were outnumbered. Sometimes, like tonight.

"Fuck 'em," the other decided as they headed to one of the wooded parts of the iconic park. It had been the scene of many crimes but none like tonight. They ended up in the exact same place five poor black kids were victimized after someone else victimized a white woman jogger.

The men on their trail peeled off their own riding suits as they walked. Six naked black men walking through Central Park may have been normal, but it was anything but when they morphed from man to beast under the light of the full moon. Four of the six were relatively new to the life and could only turn when the moon was full. That gave them three nights a month to unleash the beast. Dog and Beans were vets like their leader and could turn at will. All six transformed and trotted off in different directions to surround the prey they were hunting.

A homeless man was seeking refuge in a bottle of strong wine when he saw a huge wolf trot past. His eyes went wide at the sight, then checked his half full bottle. He decided he was where he was trying to go and screwed the top back on.

The Lycans reached their destination and laid the woman down. Neither complained when the men took position between their legs without the precaution of protection. Sleeping with strangers from a club was proof of their recklessness so what good was a rubber. The men had just entered the women when werewolves pounced from every direction.

"What the..." one of the women shrieked while the other one screamed. Two of the werewolves snatched one of the Lycans by each arm before he could transform. Dog moved in and quickly bit the back of his neck. The blow severed his spine and prevented him from changing. He clamped down even further until his head rolled away.

The other woman had seen all she needed to see and abandoned her screams. She scrambled to her feet and took off running naked through the park. The remaining woman watched in disbelief as the man who was just inside of her turned into a huge beast. More wolf than man, yet he remained upright on two feet.

The remaining Lycan unleashed a backhand blow that sent one of the werewolves sailing. He landed a hundred feet away before rolling fifty more feet. A blow from his other claw opened another werewolf's torso and exposed his ribs. A roar erupted from his fanged mouth as he took a battle stance.

Dog leapt twenty feet in the air and came down on his back. The Lycan whirled to dislodge him but another wolf clamped down on its leg. He soon had a werewolf on each limb while Beans went for his throat. The last wolf recovered from the blow and joined the pack. He bit down on the back of the Lycan's neck.

The Lycans superior strength wasn't much help against the superior numbers of the wolves. They too were relatively new to this life and got caught slipping. It was instant karma for doing exactly what their leader ordered them not to do. Their car contained enough guns and silver ammo to kill a pack of werewolves. Neither did him any good from the car. He made a break for the car but the six beast attacking him wore him down. Finally Dog and the last wolf met in the middle of his neck and severed his spine. A chorus of howls filled the night air and rippled through the trees like a sudden breeze.

The woman just blinked in disbelief at what she had just witnessed. She was only in search of some dick and ended up with an unbelievable tale to tell her friends. Or not since the wolves suddenly turned in her direction.

"No!" she screamed when most of the pack had turned in her direction. Her next scream died in her throat when Dog bit into it. Blood exploded from between his fangs and soaked his fur. The rest of the pack moved in and began to eat. Except for Beans who took off in another direction. He galloped on all four paws and took giant strides that covered thirty yards apiece.

"What the fuck! What the fuck!" the other woman repeated as she sprinted for the exit. She could see the yellow blur of taxis whipping about and almost made it. She lifted her hand to hail one just feet from the sidewalk. That was as close as she would get.

Beans snatched her into his powerful jaws and dragged her back into the park. He dropped her next to what was left of her friend. Two others joined him and pulled her apart like BBQ pork butt. They devoured the women in between howls that caused regular dogs to holla back with howls of their own

The dead Lycans slowly transformed back into mutilated men. Once the wolves were fed they turned and walked away. They too transformed back into men as they went. They caught up with their clothing and dressed before exiting the park.

"I need a cigarette," Beans chuckled as they headed back to the bikes.

"Or dessert," another joked. Meanwhile, Dog was more subdued. He let out a sigh knowing they now had to deal with Rajeem. Their leader always tried to avoid clashes with the Lycans and only he knew why.

The electric motorcycles whipped quietly down the FDR, turning heads as they rode. They sped past a police car who decided not to pursue. It was too close to shift change to get stuck filling out reports. That was as good an excuse as any since he knew his beat up patrol car couldn't catch them. They whipped by in a blur of leather while his car smoked like a Philly blunt in a project staircase.

They exited the highway at a high speed and headed over to the building. The same elevator took them up to the roof where they parked the motorcycles. Of course Rajeem smelled them when they neared the neighborhood, so he was waiting when they reached his loft.

"Sup Rajeem," Beans greeted casually as they entered.

"You gonna eat the rest of that?" one of the other werewolves asked when he saw what remained of Shontay. Rajeem quickly smelled through the distraction.

"No? No! Tell me you didn't?" Rajeem fussed when he caught the unmistakable scent of Lycan blood. He knew it better than they ever could since he was closer to any Lycan than they could ever be.

"We waited for another time, like you said," Beans offered lightly. The look on Rajeem's face quickly erased the smirk twisting the corner of his lip.

"When Arrax comes for revenge I might just let him have you," Rajeem snarled. He knew the leader of the Lycans didn't take dead Lycans lightly. Dog just shook his head and held his tongue.

"Who is Arrax?" another werewolf asked out the corner of his mouth as Rajeem and Dog stepped aside to speak privately.

"His brother," Beans replied. He knew better than most, this could be trouble.

"You think he's going to take the bait?" Dog asked. They both knew Beans would do the exact opposite of what he was told, just like Rajeem wanted him to do.

"If he doesn't we'll just keep hunting Lycans until he does!" Rajeem snarled. There was bad blood between the brothers although they had once been very close. That of course was many, many moons ago.

www.ingramcontent.com/pod-product-compliance
Lightning Source LLC
Chambersburg PA
CBHW051954220626
47052CB00004B/944